GW00696741

The Dark Side of Light

The magic of writing is when you can make the reader see a visual in his head as he reads the words. Sanil's writing has that quality. Brilliant, insightful and totally engaging.

—Piyush Pandey, Executive Chairman & Creative Director, Ogilvy & Mather, India and South Asia

The Dark Side of Light is an interesting read with its refreshingly original style of blending short stories and poems. Sanil Sachar makes his mark as a promising new age Indian author—particularly because he is young and uninhibited in expression.

—Deepak Parekh, Chairman, HDFC Limited

Sanil Sachar writes with a poet's lyricism and a philosopher's emotional maturity. *The Dark Side of Light* challenges and comforts the reader with its delightful flights, dips and surprises.

—Shoba Narayan, author of *Katha* and *Return to India*

This is a book that combines prose and poetry in a fluid manner. The journey and the search for meaning is set against the backdrop of London, Goa, Istanbul and Kargil, painting rich mosaic of culture, emotions, relationships and contemplation. Sanil writes with a flow that's involving, touching and reflective, a sheer joy from a young author.

—D. Shivakumar, Chairman and CEO, PepsiCo India

It was a delight to read Sanil's stories. It is great to see his poems and short stories together in the same book.

—Vikram Chandra, author of *Srinagar Conspiracy*, and CEO and Executive Director, NDTV Group

Sanil hones in on shades of happenings of the past and skilfully positions them into tight spaces within the present tense. He lives true to his age while exploring fantasies and illusions... His narrative is replete with creative surprises that manifest in the suspenseful unfolding of a plot.

—Muzaffar Ali, filmmaker

In this digitally hectic life, it is a treat to find a writer like Sanil. His stories have depth and simplicity at the same time, making them very engaging. The ease in his writing makes this book a lovely read.

—Neena Gupta, actress

Sanil tells his tales with great mastery over imagery, combined with a wonderful understanding of human nature. This compilation of short stories and poems is a complex honesty of the world around us, and it is quite extraordinary to see Sanil continue to grow as a writer in already his second book, at such a young age.

—Pramit Jhaveri, CEO, Citi India

The Dark Side of Light

SANIL SACHAR

RUPA

Published by
Rupa Publications India Pvt. Ltd 2016
7/16, Ansari Road, Daryaganj
New Delhi 110002

Sales Centres:

Allahabad Bengaluru Chennai
Hyderabad Jaipur Kathmandu
Kolkata Mumbai

ISBN: 978-81-291-3976-4

First impression 2016

10 9 8 7 6 5 4 3 2 1

The moral right of the author has been asserted.

Printed in India by Replika Press Pvt. Ltd.

For Sita and Sanjiv Sachar
My propellers, motivators, critics, mom and dad

There were two roads ahead, I could either go right and see what's left or I could go left and do all that's right. I created a third route and now I'm left with all that's right.
—Sanil Sachar

Contents

Acknowledgements

Firstly, I'd like to thank you for picking up *The Dark Side of Light*. This book has taken years of erased words to write each story which will help strengthen the faith you have in me and I will continue this endeavour. As you choose to lose yourself in the characters, poems and stories in store, I hope you find yourself in the journeys they have to narrate to you.

Despite writing this book, Acknowledgements is the hardest section to pen down solely because naming these key people will not justify the support they have provided to construct each page.

My sister, Shreya Sachar, whose poem I stole for a school magazine when I was eight, resulting in my initiation as a writer. Thank you for not calling plagiarism on that and the several assignments 'I did'.

The entire team at Rupa Publications. Your support reinforces me with ideas and words, strengthening this everlasting bond of ours. In particular, I'd like to thank Dibakar Ghosh for the support he has shown me ever since our first meeting in 2012. 'Keep writing and let's meet in two months,' still echo in my ears as a constant motivation.

Fiction, poetry and any form of literature is driven by personal experiences and those encountered by others around you. Therefore, my friends, who are a constant drive to my mistakes, successes, laughter, all of which are usually connected to the same events, this book is a symbol of many more such times to come.

Raghav Sikka, Rishi Jolly, Ishaan Khosla, Barun Roy Chowdhury and Sumer Bir Singh, characters in my life who constantly provide me with a wide range of characteristics and stories. Some which can be told and many which won't ever be. To complete this puzzle, the most vibrant piece, Saba Kapoor. A friendship where we know too much to get out of even if we wanted to. After reading the first draft to most of my work through messages, here is the final draft.

Adding the precise words to this book has led to several hours of consultation and debates, followed by many more hours of wasting time which ultimately led to the correct words. For that, there is Keshav Moodliar. I am waiting for the day when one of my characters is written for you to act. That day is not far.

Don't judge a book by its cover. However, many tend to, and for that reason the name of the book is one of the vital elements. A decision so high in magnitude I didn't deem myself ideal for it. Thus, the only person who holds such credibility is Izzy Squire. A woman who luckily didn't judge me by the cover when we first met is responsible for the name of this book, *The Dark Side of Light*. Her persona and presence is a predominant attribute for my work. Thank you for the book (A levels, university accommodation, university, I think you get the gist).

To conclude, the beginning and the end of each thought, my parents who have shown their faith in each of my decisions before I can. For you, this book is a mere token of my love that bears no limits.

An Eye for an Eye

'Three students found buried near the teachers' parking lot.'
'Four children found charred in a playground near school.'
'Five women found hanged with conjoined daggers holding them together.'

The obituaries were taking up more space in the papers than the matrimonials. Times were even more invaluable and the uncertainty about the next second led to anxiety about what to prioritize. Each hug before work or a kiss to a parent was treated as the last; bringing urgency into everyday emotions like affection.

Parents finally made time to play hide and seek; but this time they knew they wouldn't find the girl who used to constantly beg them to find her. Now communities and neighbours came together, caught up in this relentless search. A handkerchief attached near their dear one's beating heart was used as a navigator when their prized possession didn't return from school. The cloth stuck near their name tags was the first clue towards a nightmarish identification search. Soon, the simplicity of sending their children to school became a gamble for nervous parents.

These headlines flashed like neon lights of an ambulance as they blinded everyone with dark thoughts, erasing hope for the future. A lifetime seemed to have passed as these grotesque murders contained no clues while the killer plagued the world, causing panic. The number of murders and unsolved crimes increased as if indicating they were a means to control the population. Doors stayed locked with constant prayers for them not to be broken through. Children aren't the only ones who check under their beds for unexpected visitors and knives aren't just used as cutlery.

I often wondered what happened to murderers. What went through their minds after they ended their hunger? Do these murderers ever taste their own medicine? Why can't the news broadcast that? This curiosity began to kill me and I wasn't prepared to die.

The mind is selfish. It stores all the good thoughts deep inside, making it easier to pick out negativity from the top. We find ourselves ignoring the few seconds of happiness when our teeth are exposed to the light; completely disregarding the rare occasion when we smile. Like expecting to not feel low after being high, we demand guilty pleasures without any consequences. Decades are spent finding the meaning of life when survival is the only answer. To exist is to contribute, however positive or negative that might be. Taking away the meaning of life or life itself is a sinful dictatorship many falsely believe they possess. If you can't help someone survive then you have no right to cut the source that enables them to keep solving this puzzle.

We all have a moment where we are pushed to the limits. Some are shoved; while most run into the wall fast enough for the pain to numb the sensation that overpowers us. A sense that leads you to drown yourself or tie stones to others as you push them. I had reached that level of insanity. We aren't here long enough to be good at everything; we need to be wise and cunning. As Mahatma Gandhi said, 'We need to be the change we wish to see'. You need to pick where you are king and that's what I did.

Like derby horses, we wear blinders against the evil and look at the brighter side of life. The smoke in the air is embraced as clouds. The echoing screams are taken to be children playing games in a park and the road not taken is trusted. Shaken up by these ghastly events in the present, we stop believing in the future we lie to our children about. The days are darker than the nights and we have started to fear living as much as we fear death. Our lives are not in our hands. They are controlled by some unseen force, trying to force us to live as long as we can. We're born and we're taught how to live and as soon as we get older we're told to make a living and not a life. We are told more things than we are asked. Even as we get older, the options around us increase but like empty boxes in a store room, only one box might have something we want. One is not a choice, yet we are conned into believing we are independent.

I often wondered who would describe the suspect to the sketch artist when there was no witness to the crime. If there was a witness, then surely they should be the suspect as well. All the sketches that had been put up around the town resembled movie posters. Monetary rewards under each name, putting a price on lives that were taken. Soon each life lost was given a retail price. Every black and white drawing stuck on dimly lit lamp posts had a common feature. They all had a smile on their faces. Some smiles could be seen in the eyes while the most blatant ones were on the faces, rejoicing in achieving their selfish act. They all looked like each other. Like me or anyone else on the street. It was only a matter of where to start cleaning up. I couldn't let them win and get their way. I had to prevent them from quenching their thirst, so they eventually die of starvation.

I was lost in my own game of hide and seek, persistent in finding my wife and daughter ever since the night of our little mirror reflection's recital. She had been ecstatic and apprehensive to be on stage while addressing a hundred audience members as she was going to sing her over-rehearsed lullaby. I wish I had hugged her tighter, hard enough to not let go. Now I walk out of my room waiting for her to jump out to scare me but the silence is my biggest fear. Like her, I constantly practice each lullaby with the hopeless faith that I will get to serenade the one I love, performing my best. But my courage is often overshadowed by my insanity. If only she knew today that her wish of attracting a large crowd has come true, in a very different way. What kills me is the mystery behind this lost cause. Like climbing a slide I find myself slipping faster every time I try to climb it quicker. I fall fast, attempting to answer these unwanted questions. I have been deprived of the two people for whom my heart beat equally. I walk down streets trying to identify those who took away my reason to smile. Every person on the pavement looks the same; they all look like killers. It makes me question why we are born if we are not even given the right to choose when to leave?

Today was a fresh start in my life. I felt like a gladiator entering the arena for the first time. Fierce and nervous, I wanted to make a lasting impression onto a life I adopted while I held that 9 mm black pistol, with an ecstatic expression on my face. He sat soaked in his crushed white shirt that was transparent with the buckets of sweat his trembling body produced. I put the pistol to his head. He shook like a leaf. Sitting in his office cabin where he was king during office hours, I felt like a lion ruling over his territory. His torso remained tied to the chair he usually pretended to be working on. I took aim with the tip of the gun that became moist as it was held against his temple, waiting for him to scream loud enough to compete with the noise of the revolver. My fingers felt more comfortable on the trigger than they did when I had held my wife's face to kiss her before she left for the recital. We all go through a struggle to live, so we definitely deserved a fight to die. I stood with the nozzle staring at him, as it soon got prepared to take away his right to breathe; the one act we are allowed to perform without consent. There were twenty minutes left for the next day to flash news of newer crimes and I felt responsible for preventing him from hearing such atrocities.

Yesterday's work echoed in my ear as it was a fresh day but my new interest led me to the same schedule, with a different person. I made her sit down on a chair too. She had a long way to go in life but time had run out. I wanted her to be comfortable. Nothing can be compared to a comfortable death and she deserved a memorable farewell. Her expression was much like the man's, mirroring the grim expressions I saw. Her insides were on fire and she would soon be, too; the moment she chose to stop breathing. Nothing comes easily in life and there is no better example than life itself. She sat soaked in kerosene while a candle was lit; it came steadily closer to her mouth, waiting to perform the last rites. Her lips, salted, with tears that fell from eyes that were staring straight at the fire; it reflected a hazy image of herself. She quivered with her body reaching a state of shock reminding me that in the end, fear is the fundamental emotion that stays till the very last second. I didn't want her to plead for her life because no life that you beg for is worth living for. I wanted her to earn a prolonged life.

Tonight I worked under the light of the moon that added beauty to my work. My new canvas was a man seated like a passenger on a plane about to crash. I respected him enough to prepare his coffin prior to the estimated time of departure.

With his feet hanging just above the ground he was going to be buried under. He shuffled about digging his own grave with each movement that ploughed the coffin into the mud, with the help of its sharp corners. His eyes said more to me than his gagged mouth could, as we both sat opposite each other waiting for the show to end. He had a striking similarity to my earlier victims, who lost fighting as death kidnapped them. He begged; at first it was for his life and then, in complete contrast, he couldn't wait to die. Digging his own grave with each vigorous movement of the coffin he was tied to as he waited to be buried. His eyes seemed to be screaming but there was no sound while he dug his way to eternal silence.

We all are scared of death but there is a part of our mind that knows how to accept it when there is no other option. A mechanism takes over that aids us to endure the pain that precedes death. Useless thoughts and feelings occur. Each one of my subjects accepted their body as the canvas when different shades of red stained them, making my job easier.

Today I planned a new activity for myself. This one was more challenging with twice the number of participants in this game to live. I was a spectator watching them communicate as they mumbled, gagging on the hollow pipes that were connected to their identical mouths. In school I had learned that twins could communicate with each other through cryptophasia and I could see this private language at play as their tears streamed down in sync. With their backs to each other, their lives depended on one another. This life was a selfish act and these twins were put to an unselfish test. Bound together once again they sat close, tied by ropes that were covered with blades. A movement too sharp and uncoordinated and the blade would cut their wrists; a movement too slow would continue the slow torture they put themselves through my masterpiece. I witnessed teamwork at its finest as they synced their movement and managed their breathing perfectly to keep each other alive. But like every partnership, this one would come to an end as well. The serrations on the blades were finely carved, adding a touch of class to their death. A lax movement from either side and one of the many blades situated a centimetre away from their body would do the job of a barb on a fishing hook. They were mirror reflections of each other with birth marks on the exact opposite sides of their body and I provided them with the opportunity to deepen this similarity with identical scars. My generosity gifted these brothers with an opportunity to depart together just so they didn't have to feel incomplete. My charitable masterpiece deserved more than the one audience member. Yet again, I was a spectator to the acceptance of faith; in unison they welcomed the end.

Over time, I realized death isn't any fun if you can't see it coming. They all had an expression of relief on their faces right before they knew it was time to depart. A sense of achievement appeared in their eyes just before they closed for eternity. I helped each of them to feel an array of emotions; that's what added to the kindness of each deed. With the concentration of a surgeon, I continued my pursuit of restricting murderers from conducting their practice. I was a proud artist, subtle in my work and deprived of recognition. My favourite part was not the killing but the finale. I lived for those moments when death was accepted as a blessing because they decided when it would be. Like a magician, my trick was not finished until the climax; in this case it wasn't until I made the body disappear.

We are all the same. We are all survivors. We are all killers. My actions wouldn't bring back those who had been taken away but it would bring the rest of them together. By the end that's where we all will be and that will be our world. I am essentially helping the cause we are forced to be a part of. I couldn't bear the lack of respect people had for another's life. I was a martyr providing others with an opportunity to soak in the fact that death will be the wiser option. I never lost sleep because of my day's activities; simply because I was a part of a nightmare even when I was awake. And when you're an insomniac, there is no difference. Silence is not the answer to quench this undisputed thirst to kill and we all learn it the hard way. An eye for an eye was the answer.

An Itch Within

A sensation, it builds from the bottom of my spine,
Makes its way up my shoulder blades,
This itch is giving me a sign.

I remove my jumper and every other piece of clothing,
That gets me to see,
The itch isn't in my back,
It's all those thoughts I've stacked.

Ruminations that are crawling their way out,
What feels like an irritation on top of my skin,
Is the anxiety and pain accumulating within.

I cry a scream of anguish, with a desperate sense of wonder,
What is this itch that makes me want to tear till down under?
Is it anxiety caused from far-fetched goals?
Or is it that while I try and sew up my life,
I constantly create holes?

The irritation starts to build from the bottom of my feet,
I claw through my socks only to cause a bleed,
But this unwanted sensation finds another destination,
Forever raging me to tear into my skin,
Leading to my own desolation.

State of Desolation

Turn the tap to the right,
Nothing flows out.
You turn it again,
The same outcome.
You give out a loud shout.

Looking under the pillows,
Checking impatiently under the bed,
Desperately looking for the key, as you turn red.

You close your eyes,
At least your unconscious self won't bring you down.
You find yourself being pushed in an empty pool,
Not a drop of water, yet your imagination makes you drown.

Everything seems to flow in the opposite direction,
Even the blade becomes blunt,
Just to make you face all the brunt,
It's like you're alone in your very own secluded section.

Unsurprisingly fed up, you walk to turn off the lights,
To find they were never on.
Frustrated, you try to tie the noose,
To see even the ceiling has gone.

Nothing works in your favour,

You look up for a saviour,
And see the ground staring back at you.

You begin to hallucinate,
Only to realize, that the rest was indeed reality,
You weep as you hope for these illusions to fade away,
As they evaporate with your sanity.

End

I hear voices in the dark,
I see shadows around me in the day,
I feel the raindrops trickle down my face,
And yet I don't feel alive.

I look for peace in the busiest places,
I look at mirrors and only see shattered faces,
Words flow easier when they are constrained within,
I can sense the end approach,
Although I am yet to begin.

Successful Rejection

$\mathcal{D}$ressed in a suit and feeling confident, I sit answering promptly as though I have formulated the questions. Responding with utmost sincerity, replying as if reading out vows, with the hope that an affirmative nod is the reply from the other side. Each door I have entered has opened to another leading to the same questions I have mastered responses to; just not the correct ones. I've become an actor with the mirror as my most loyal audience, constantly practicing expressions and replies, ultimately deceiving myself into believing this sense of satisfaction is real.

'*How many golf balls can fit into this room?*'

'*That depends on their size.*'

'*How many humans can fit into this room?*'

'*That depends on their size.*'

'*How many pay cheques can fit into this room?*'

'*That depends on… Well, maybe as many as you can write.*'

Back and forth these questions are fired like throwing a ball at a wall. I sit with a poker face, with my feelings disguised.

'*What made you choose this company?*'

'*What made you choose this line of business?*'

'*What made you study at Delhi University?*'

The questions are asked with the tempo increasing with each syllable as I sit focusing on the keywords in order to pretend to understand. I face constant rejection as I continue to knock and walk through doors with the hope that I can fit into society's norm of what is well off and successful. But my knuckles and my self-confidence face constant bruises with each new knock.

'You don't have enough experience.'

'We're looking for someone younger.'

'You don't have enough experience.'

'We're looking for someone younger.'

'You don't have enough experience.'

'We're looking for...'

Sounding like the alarm that screeches to wake me up each morning so I can walk through a door to hear rejections, these justifications are spat on me with unfortunate familiarity.

There are days the tie I wear like a noose waiting to be tugged at is less suffocating than the spacious cabins I aspire to call my second home. These chambers have rejected me from entering them; but persistence will pay off is a lie I convince myself like a mantra.

When I initially signed up for these sittings of torture that exhaust motivation, I used to feel nervous. Apprehensive purely because I didn't want to seem imperfect. Reading notes countless times, over and over and over again, chanting them like a prayer. Now I sing these lines internally; they are like an infectious song stuck in my head, causing my brain to feel parched. I was afraid of being imperfect, only to be reassured each time that perfection was a goal too far-fetched for someone as disoriented as I was. Now as I enter these rooms, I play a game with myself. This way, I'll win something. I challenge myself into predicting the layout of the room I will be brought into as I am asked questions that will not be associated with the job. The smaller the room, the stricter and the fiercer the interviewer and the questions are even more unrelated to the job profile. I feel like I am addicted to rejection. I wouldn't know what to do if I was selected. I enter with the aim of securing the position but my comfort towards rejection pleads I fail, again.

I had dreamt of this day, however vivid and unclear. This time, I shook his hand only at the start but the end was different from how it panned out every time; and that's what made this dream difficult to forget.

'Looking for an enthusiastic, hard-working professional.'

'Looking for a goal driven team leader with ambitions of growth in the industry.'

'Looking for...'

These printed adverts play hide and seek, forever making me chase each job I cut and paste in my internal bank of aspirations. Like a schizophrenic I pretend to be ambitious in every sector of business but persistence doesn't pay off. Often reminded we are all fighting our own battles, I am frequently convinced I am a sheep for the slaughter in a world full of carnivores slowly building an appetite.

Over-qualified with degrees that did not interest my employer, certain job descriptions that demanded an aesthetic physical appearance immediately restricted my entry. These days, when I failed the least was when I felt the most victorious.

The moment I'd enter the buildings which paid salaries that were nullified by taxes, my facial muscles were used to forming a smile. This pretense appreciation was replicated by several more clones waiting to be called to be tested, seated on uncomfortable chairs under rickety, unstable fans. Our similar attires and nervous smiles, while we clutched onto our CV's, made us all emulations of one another. There were days when one of them would walk out with a smile so unfamiliar to my eyes, making it certain that the rest of us who were sitting were there for a mere formality. Yet I repeated my rehearsed answers like a broken record with hope, a feeling that was slowly becoming alien to me.

This was the furthest I had ever gotten. I still felt nervous and terrified of the uncertain success that could occur. The room in which a man in a suit analysed every action, made me speak slower than I usually would. The atmosphere was tense enough and made it difficult for me to look even a few feet beyond the chair I felt glued to.

'Why do you want this job?'

'What makes you different?'

'Why should we hire you?'

The questions asked were similar to every interview I had failed; but this time it felt I was hearing another voice for the first time. The truth is the best option forward because it always remains the same. At least that's the mantra I used to follow before this test and the outcome never took me beyond, *'We regret to inform you that you have not been selected.'* This time I rehearsed each answer enough times to be brainwashed into believing it was the truth.

The interviewer's mahogany desk had papers stacked neatly on it. They were weighed down by a handmade paper weight, presumably made by the young child whose picture was a decoration on a silver photo frame. All this accompanied by a hot cup of coffee were all components of the life I envied. The interviewer's tall, upright frame made me feel insecure. My crumpled over used shirt was an embarrassment compared to his ironed sky blue shirt complimented by a blazer. He was awfully kind and listened to every answer I gave to his question; all these attributes made me dislike him even more. The absurdity of his acceptance resulted my being reflexively defensive.

'You're the perfect candidate for this job. Your answers to each question reinstate my confidence in your ability to help this company

grow along with your own personal strengths; we would love for you to be a part of this firm. HR will take the paperwork forward and we'd be glad to have you work with us.'

Dumbfound by his offer I stood dazed, gazing mutely at him.

'How many prisoners can you fit in a prison cell?' I responded in a deadpan voice.

'Depends on the size of the prison,' he reasoned, with animated hand gestures mimicking being in a prison cell.

'No, it depends on the crime.'

Those were the last words we exchanged as I stood up to strangle him. As his unblinking eyes began to protrude, he wore the same expression of concentration as he analysed my performance; I decided his fate this time. Never before had I felt so much in control; the power that was in my hands was too overwhelming for me to savour slowly. Only a few minutes back I sat choked up about what lay ahead and here I was standing where he sat, watching as he choked on the tie stuffed into his mouth restricting his entry into the future. Overthinking only leads you to believe the rubbish that stays in your head the longest. I hated over-complicating my life and I absolutely despised not knowing what to do because it complicated my existence. This man had tried pushing me out of my comfort zone. I loved sitting on the other side of the table trying to get rid of the questions thrown at me like javelins; it was my job to protect my life.

Three Hundred Ticks of the Clock

I've been holding this pen,
For over three hundred ticks of the clock,
Staring at our display picture, hoping it would talk.
And teach me how I could go back in time,
And change every moment I made the same smile,
That is now a distant memory, vanish.
To each time you'd say a few words in French,
And I'd try to match up to you,
With my one-word knowledge in Spanish.

I start to draw her sweet honey-coated gold tresses,
Which cascades over her contagious smile,
With the hope that those familiar lips move,
And start to speak,
Even if it were for a short while.

I close my eyes as I start to draw yours now,
Ever so clear in my head.
I know the exact proportion of each of your brows,
Of each lash that would act as a shutter that retracted,
When I narrated a rehearsed joke,
You always told me it's best when I think less,
And that's exactly what I'm trying to do now.

Painful Comfort

I've felt this prick that many yearn for,
I've been pierced by the sensation,
That umpteen pretend to medicate themselves with.

I seek for a cure from this catalyst,
That has several knock-off versions,
I seek serenity from this chaotic sensation,
That rushes like cocaine through my numb body,
That feels like a jab with each beat as it pierces deeper,
To comfort me from the constant reminder,
That it is here to stay.

I have felt it once and now I know why once is enough,
Now I know why it is a drug,
Now I know why we are all dealers and addicts,
Now I know it is the only pain that soothes.
Now I know its name.

Tamanna

I wondered why I was in this state. Why I was in such pain? Why had I let it all happen to me when I could have avoided it? Then the reason acted like anaesthesia; it eclipsed the pain and calmed me down so I could embark on a path I adamantly chose to take. When something you could die for takes you away, are you defeated or victorious?

I never understood why they asked us what we wanted to become when we grew up, year after year at school. What I found even more absurd was that with each passing year most of my friends would change what they wanted to be. I made up my mind as soon as I was gifted my first set of G.I. Joe action figures. From that moment I wanted to be not just a mere object but a protector of my country. As I grew older, I started to realize the army was the closest I'd get to achieve my ambition; till the day I enrolled in the army at the age of 21, I dedicated every bit of myself to achieve my goal. Yes, she played a vital role in it. I did love her, I respected her, and I owed a lot to her, if not everything; and if there was anything I'd die for, it was her. I owed everything to my country, thus being her protector was my primary aim and my way of repaying her for giving me a home.

Going against my family's wishes, when I enrolled I had to give up a major part of myself for something I truly desired and loved; thus being sent off to a village near Ladakh was more mentally than physically taxing. The cold was at times unbearable and the constant risk of bomb blasts was a continuous threat to each one of us out there. I was in such awe of the idea of serving my country that the thought of death was something that never crossed my mind, a fear I was oblivious to. It all changed in a flash; maybe it was because I had focused all my emotions on being a soldier that when they deviated slightly, I was caught entirely off guard and fell straight into this trap I was completely unprepared for.

As I sat there off duty, she approached me with two cups of coffee in her hand and handed one to me. Her warmth and her presence seemed much more effective than the coffee. Her face, fresher than the morning snow and eyes the colour of the dark roasted coffee beans used to brew what was on store. I didn't ask her her name and she never asked mine for some reason, but every morning at five she would hand me a hot cup of coffee and speak to me about everything but my job. It had been just over six months and we'd meet each other for half an hour till the break of dawn, after which she would have to leave. I stopped myself from asking her her name or any details about her personal life because I knew I was not capable of dividing my emotions between my job and someone as beautiful and kind as her. I was certainly not strong enough to get myself out of what I was falling into and that played a major part in resisting myself from getting to know her any better.

It was in the middle of January in 1997 that I got my first call to serve my country at Kargil; this battlefield is where I learned more about my duties and surprisingly, about myself and my new desire. Living in those trenches, hours of shelter in the dark, turning into a constant exchange of bullets across the border, as if reminding the other side of one's presence, was a slow and terrible wait for a few peaceful minutes. I made it a point not to get too close to my companions because, as soldiers, each second we lived was an extra moment of being blessed; we all knew how limited these blessings were in our line of work. I saw many fall, even more stand tall and protect the land they stood on. I too was one of them, fearless about my mortality, until I felt that shell sink right through my shoulder blades, followed by an excruciating pain in my upper body as I was flung several feet away from one of our trenches, which were left in ruins with many of my fellow companions whose blessings came crashing down as well. The pain I felt cannot be described but the realization that I would not be able to see her made me recover much faster in the hospital. I knew I wanted to go back to the border as soon as I felt fit enough to, but before that I had to go back to see her. Maybe the abruptness of how I had to leave a year and a half ago made me even more eager to go back to sipping yet another coffee with her or go back there and know when our last time together would be.

After counting four slowly passing months in the hospital, I decided to go back to Ladakh. It was colder and mistier than usual, I was going back after over a year but the place seemed almost entirely different, unusually quiet and quite eerie. I went back to my base camp which was a few kilometres away from where she and I used to meet in the mornings. I went back to that same spot and it didn't appear anything like it had; the land seemed completely ploughed and the houses nearby seemed to have been demolished. I couldn't do anything to clear my confusion so I went back to my base camp, where a letter with my name on it was waiting for me. It was dated approximately four months from that day and having never received a letter from anyone before, this seemed rather unusual.

I lost my husband today in a bomb blast in Kargil. He was a brave man and I am sure you are too. We were married for less than a year, that too, against our families' wishes. I know you and I spoke every morning for several months but I am certain you didn't know any of this or that I am originally from Karachi. In order to marry a man from the neighbouring country when times are so cruel, elopement was the only way forward. Maybe separating us was Allah's way of punishment. I don't know whether you are alive or with my husband now but I just thought I'd let you know that you were a very dear friend to me even though we didn't know each other well and I thank you for being there for me when he wasn't.

—Tamanna

It all seemed too much for me. I didn't know whether I was more upset about her loss or the fact that I wasn't there for her while he was at war. Or maybe I was disappointed in myself for getting into something that could not go anywhere and yet I found it terribly difficult to get out of. The returning address of the letter was a primary school which was approximately eighteen kilometres away from where I was. The first thing I did in the morning was set out to meet Tamanna and let her know that I was alive and whatever else I could build up the courage to say. When I got there, all I could see was a demolished building with bits of glass scattered everywhere and heaps of dirt around it. It had clearly been struck by a terrible bomb blast. Behind it all was a small shed under which sat a group of twenty children being taught by a girl who seemed no older than sixteen. I waited for forty-five minutes only to be told by the 16-year-old that Tamanna had been forced to go back to Karachi after her family had learned that she had been widowed. She was now getting married to a soldier named Lance Naik Salim Ibraham. The girl also told me that Tamanna was even more disheartened about being sent into the house of another member of the army. It was an idea that had caused her enough pain that she had lost the power to fight against her family's wish. After the young teenager learned of my one-sided love for Tamanna, she let me keep a picture sent by Tamanna, of herself and Lance Naik Ibrahim, on the day of their engagement. Tamanna's remorse and disapproval was concealed by the makeup she wore. She looked like the most beautiful bride-to-be, and I wished I was in the picture with her. I decided from that moment I wouldn't try and contact her or act as a hindrance in her life in any way. I would devote myself entirely to the army.

It was the first week of May 1999 and I, along with hundreds of others, was ordered to report back to Kargil where the conflict between India and Pakistan had gotten severe; shells upon shells of ammunition had been lobbed against one another. The Kargil War was at its most brutal stage. Nevertheless the bullets and sacrifices around me didn't prevent me from constantly thinking of yet another morning encounter with her in the future. These daydreams would be obstructed by the image of a tall, well-built soldier in a camouflage uniform, who was soon to be her husband. I often thought I was losing my mind over someone who didn't have any feelings for me but instead only spoke to me because my profession reminded her of the husband she didn't get to spend enough time with. But then, does love always have to be mutual for it to be real?

I was put in charge of my trench and we were assigned to reclaim our bases which had been taken over by the Pak Fauj. The dust in the air had accumulated over several days, mixed with the heat from the numerous blasts taking place at irregular intervals around us; it almost made it impossible to see. The sounds of bullets and the cries of the wounded seemed to follow us on our way to the base camp we endeavoured to win back. We set up our spots. Being in charge made me responsible not only for the well-being of my country but also for the men who were following my commands. All this responsibility helped dull the thought of Tamanna and the abrupt ending of a story that had never begun.

We moved forward slowly as we used bullet upon bullet to advance further to reclaim the area that was ours. That was until we reached a turn which seemed very quiet. This almost made it seem like we had fully reclaimed our camp, taking down each of the soldiers that appeared as a hindrance. Despite the impending feeling of achievement, we had to make sure the last bend was clear in order to be completely certain of our accomplishment. Being the commander, I chose to move forward in order to prevent jeopardizing the lives of my fellow soldiers. As I took the turn I tried looking through all the ash and dust, through which I could see a figure, almost like my reflection, trying to sneak across the other side of the border in order to protect himself. Just before I chose to pull the trigger, I got a clearer picture of this camouflaged soldier. After recognizing him, I pulled my finger away from the trigger and informed the rest of the soldiers that we could go back to our original trenches as we had secured the location. I had promised myself that I would not be a hindrance to Tamanna and I could definitely not let her grieve over the same thing twice. So I turned my back to let him slip away. Realizing what I had done, I felt my awareness kick in, instigating a burning sensation in my gut. The feeling was multiplied after I was shot just where that sensation had emerged from. I don't know what happened after my eyes closed. I don't know whether Tamanna went back to teaching or if Salim was there for coffee with her every morning. But

I know I would have done the same if I was in his place, just to be able to stand next to her at the altar. I guess that's what made me go with a smile on my face and her name on my lips.

So when I wondered why I was in this state? Why I was enduring such pain? Why I let it all happen to me, when I could avoid this situation? I let the reason act as an anaesthesia to eclipse the pain and calm me in order for me to go down a road I had adamantly chosen to follow. When something you could die for takes you away, is it your defeat or victory?

Reflection Fading on Me

Staring at my phone,
I feel so alone and I see you there.
Telling me I'm late,
And how you've already finished one plate.
And I realize that all these times are here in words,
That's where they'll stay.
Here I sit miles away,
Far from our favourite buffets.

I hear you telling me that I'm a fool,
For copying all your work to pass boarding school.
These messages help me fight,
Fight all these thoughts that tell me you're not here,
You're not here, I'm not there,
This isn't how I was supposed to fare.

For you I came, for you I knew,
All that I wanted to do.
Now I see my reflection is fading on me,
And I know you're the reason I will have to go,
Far, far above all these stars,
And now I feel, those times, coming back for me and you.

Distant Closeness

We sat on either sides of the world, separated by our screens and the distance. Our fingers worked, as our brains painted an image of the other, groggy, eyes half open. The sun shone brightly for her, while it hid from me, the moon peeping from behind clouds outside my window, 7,480 miles away from her.

I have developed a deep burning desire for words that are typed from in front of a monitor which reflects my own etched reflection. From the poetry she has recited during slam competitions that attracted each listener's senses solely to her beauty wrapped in half-rhymed life experiences. To her humour; she was the loudest to laugh because she had learned to love each moment to the fullest, just so the following moments would also match up.

For hours we debated our ideas about ancient poets, with my beliefs usually backed up by a mere copy and paste off the internet so she would stay online for a few extra minutes. Her love for poetry was directly proportional to my use of the same rhythmic pentameter I swore by. We shared all our emotions with each other, forever counselling with words of wisdom we would later use to write our unread work. On days we both had spent staring at blank pages while the ink in our pens was unused and dry, we discussed methods of inspiration and mediums to stir up a conversation within our own minds. She often told me each writer has a reason, a drug that motivates the work that represents them. It was not always the kind of drug you can purchase on the streets but one that can never be banned, despite its consequences. At times our writings were a balm to medicate anguish or past moments of glee. Coleridge, for instance relied on opium to introduce the Romantic Age in English Literature. This often made me question whether opium aided in revealing the truth or whether it was a means to construct a false sense of love, a drug one would usually tend to overdose on. I am yet to develop a craving for the substance that gives me those moments of euphoria that seem to last an eternity. We are all dealers and addicts of this emotion that is shared scarcely but completely.

The unending distance between us was an obstacle to celebrating our shared passions. Our hobbies and passions were cheap and mostly free to embrace. However, we were far beyond our means to share them together. Yet, like a true cinematic cliché we were revolting against, the two of us spent the same day in art museums, just so we could compare our shared preferences and more importantly, argue about our differences, to make this distant attraction feel as normal as possible.

I'd often listen to her podcasts to find references to our discussions. Those were the days I wrote the most.

No distance is large enough to keep two similar minds away from one another. There are times when I'm in bed thinking how life would pan out if there was no distance; but then there is a mechanism in my mind that causes me to lie to myself just so I can look forward to a moment of happiness that might never show up. I often lay awake mentally sketching the moment we finally meet but there were no words that would be said in this hypothetical moment, although words had brought us together. As if it was a pantomime, I could picture her face and body move silently with only body language expressing our emotions. If we were to ever meet, I wish it was at a library, in the poetry section, amidst shelves where we could get lost trying to find our way amongst the metaphors. I can only hope she'd study me with the same passion and gratitude she analyses each book she dedicates her time to; and with confusion, too, because no book is ever perfect. In these chapters we type through silent typed conversations, I hope to add one where we meet in a library. We will be around what we love the most and again, we won't speak a word.

We met through our shared interests in how literature brings people together, and were the epitome of how distance is not an obstacle to shared passions. Nevertheless, there are days I am envious of the sun that gets to see her each morning, while all I know of her appearance is what I mentally construct based on her words. The distance between us becomes less with each passing day, when we sit on either side of the world at our scheduled time. Neither of us is fond of routine, however, this is the one exception we make and so the intimacy of our thoughts lessens the distance between us.

I find the idea of love to be rather absurd. It's like standing by the sea on a nice sunny day and you see a wave coming towards you but you keep standing there though this wave could potentially pull you in. Neither of us can say we're in love. However, if love was defined as two people who have absolute admiration for each other then we were as much in love as a couple when they first hold their newborn child. This mutual understanding was sparked over time. We weren't fools to walk into a dead end but what made us foolish was that in spite of knowing there was no future, we still chose to run into it.

Today, she hasn't appeared online and she is usually annoyingly punctual. I wait, trying to solve puzzles and taking quizzes related to ancient literature in order to test her as a connoisseur in her own expertise, when it was her who would tutor me.

Three days have passed and I wished we hadn't made the rule of not exchanging phone numbers because I haven't written anything for over seventy-two hours. I haven't thought of writing. My imagination has dried up and my fingers itch like an addict without a needle, trembling impatiently, waiting to type everything I have mentally come up with.

She no longer posts on her page. I've repeatedly listened to her previous podcasts enough to know which sentence she stuttered during and when she blushed while talking, realizing her rare mistake. Now my mind has never imagined as much and my hands have never written with so many pens. I guess she was right again. Each writer has a reason for their work; I found mine the moment I lost her.

Nights Pass By

Nights pass by, days pause and wait,
I lay here resting my thoughts,
While my eyes are wide awake.

I feel a heat in my stomach.
This isn't one from delusional fixations,
I feel a lull in my mind,
This isn't from past conversations.

My brows act as shutters,
Weighing pressure on my swollen eyes,
My mind plays the job of a bank,
Storing missed opportunities and broken lies.

I type each word,
With an anchor chained around my mouth,
Words seem to flow easier through this keyboard,
While I try and figure what I am about.

Confusion and anguish accompany me,
As subjects to my demise,
I smile at distant mirrors,
To hear back their cries.

Sudden Visitor

I hear an intruder walk up behind me.
Silent footsteps, cold winds whisper their arrival in my ear.

I look around, and feel arms lift me,
Whilst my body remains still,
Reality has never seemed so unreal to me,
As darkness begins to instill itself.

The voice, now clearer, introduces itself to me.
Covered in black from head to toe,
He explains no shadow has followed him for eternity.

'I come to you, before you could come to me,
I'll guide you well,
Past the gates of immortality.

For most die around the fear of my presence,
You have been brave to wait for me,
To guide you to your private pleasance.'

Icy breaths send chills down my spine,
As my body loses its sensations,
And numbness becomes my only ally.

'Come, my friend,
For I am only delegated to carry you to the Garden of Death,
How you would like to survive here is up to you.'

Diary of a Psychopath

Dear Diary,

The textbooks states that a psychopath is, 'someone who is characterized by an abnormal lack of empathy combined with strongly amoral conduct, masked by an ability to appear outwardly normal.'

I am a 32-year-old woman and I am normal.

Arjun, my husband, is crazy and I think he is having an affair with Neha. He says he works in a law firm; I've never asked him which and where, though.

I don't know Neha's whereabouts; some people say she was murdered.

I'm not crazy! Arjun keeps warning and reminding his friends that I'm crazy and thinks I never hear him say it; but the truth is I do and I am not. I am not crazy. We just shifted into our new apartment here in Noida. I prefer our old house; it had fewer windows and wasn't centrally located like this one. I don't like the location and how people keep welcoming us into the building. It always seems like they are trying to intrude into our lives; as if we don't have enough problems already. Arjun has called me a psychotic to my face many times and tells me I don't belong here and that my real home should be a mental asylum. I smile at him but deep inside it makes me hate him. I can't go against his word, he's all I have and I love him.

The walls in this house scare me; the colours are too bright and they seem so alive, as if they are trying to talk to me. I wonder what they want to tell me. Arjun often tells me to do something creative. He says it will cure my illness; but whenever I write in this diary he tries to take it away and says it encourages my insanity. I love Neha. She was really nice to me in college, and I often wonder how and where she is nowadays. We live on the fourth floor in our building. I love leaning against the railing in our balcony and looking down; it gives me ideas...I wonder why Arjun made us buy a home with a balcony built like a cage though? He doesn't understand me. I don't understand why we even got married. I think he's the one who needs to be in an asylum.

The house is really nice; I think I am used to it now. The walls seem friendly and I love peeping through the keyhole to see what the neighbours are up to. We have been married for a long time now; three months! Arjun says I've been going through trauma after my best friend Neha was murdered by her husband.

I'll share a secret with you. Please don't tell anybody. I killed Neha. I know she befriended me only because she wanted my Arjun! And I don't get why her husband was given the credit. I too was at the dinner. Why doesn't anybody ever pay attention to me? Why do they never applaud my work?

My pyschosis or has become severe and I can hear these voices in my head as if Neha is calling me. I love Arjun and I took his advice; I did something creative by painting our room. He came back from work and I was very excited to see his reaction. When he walked in our room he freaked out! He didn't appreciate that I had painted the whole room black. Or maybe he didn't like Neha's side of the painting. I told her he wouldn't but she never spoke back. I think he shouted at me about it because he was stressed about work. He told me

I had problems. That hurt me, so I walked out and sat in the living room.

I don't get why it's called a living room; it sounds creepy.

I heard him on the phone. I think he was talking to a client; but then I wondered if it were to the asylum, telling them to come and take me. I panicked. I didn't want to go. I didn't want to leave Arjun. I loved him. I couldn't control my emotions so I walked into the room and buried a knife in his back several times and told him to say hi to Neha from me.

I prefer this place better; it has fewer windows. They call it the asylum.

It makes me feel lonely and people look at me as if I am crazy.

I am not crazy.

Satan's Ally

Everyone has a story untold,
Nobody here is perfect,
Maybe the good are judged because they do less evil,
Everyone has their secrets.

We're all Satan's accomplices,
We'll all reunite at the end,
So is there no place like heaven?
Is it just a made up name?
Maybe, it was concocted as part of Satan's game.

Not everyone is the Devil,
But we all have a little of him in us.
Maybe that's why evil is the mirror reflection to live,
Just as our reflections are who we are.

Our shadows are the pain we have caused,
And the lies we have said.
To live one has to be evil,
We all have demon's in our head.

Trade

I always planned a certain path,
A particular route,
An ideal start.

Never did I imagine the distance it would create,
As I start pushing open,
The other path subtly starts to fade.

Was this the correct decision to make?
Was this a selfish choice that was really a mistake?

These are answers that I know I can fill in,
With the desire that is locked within.

But I am certain,
These aspirations have been ignited,
With the shared exhilaration,
So I'll do all I can to increase my motivation.
And when tomorrow, the past knocks on my door,
I hope to achieve what got me here,
Along with all that is in store.

Rubik's Cube

*L*ife is a puzzle; actually, I can solve puzzles, so let me say life is a Rubik's cube. Only a few people can get all the colours to line up; the rest, however, give up and throw it away. I am one of the latter.

I was always fascinated by high-rise buildings. The thought of being on top of the world intrigued me, even if it was only for a short while. I often went into the closed doors of offices just for a while, to look out over all the others solving their Rubik's cubes.

On 16 June 2014, I turned 22 years old and another colour was added to my complex cube; I was on the verge of ending it. But sometimes there is light at the end of the darkest tunnel and that's exactly what happened. I thought I had almost solved my Rubik's cube. I almost had every question mark answered. I almost smiled for ten seconds without faking it. But alas, almost wasn't good enough.

I was supposed to go out with her; she cheated on me. I was supposed to start my job; the company went bankrupt and fired me even before I could have my brand new shirt ironed. I couldn't wish the man I saw in the mirror well because he couldn't tick off even one goal like he had promised me he would exactly a year ago. I despised him.

I was called to the twenty-eight storey building that had to *'let me go'* exactly two weeks after hiring me, even before I could start the five-day-a-week monotonous journey. I was made to sign my resignation and in return they gifted me three months' salary as compensation, a rough sympathetic hug and a pat on the back as a consolation for my failure.

I thought I had solved my Rubik's cube only a few hours ago; then another colour was added. Now it seems like a million of them have been thrown straight at me.

I stuck to my regime of being on top of the world for at least a bit and went into the restricted area of the very office that had stopped me from joining them. To add salt to my wounds, the sun was beaming, the clouds were clear and, to everyone's surprise, the city was not being serenaded by the sound of construction. It was the ideal day to be screwed over so bad that I started to wonder whether this was all just a prank played to lead up to a surprise party at the end of the day. How I wished someone would just come out with a camera and tell me this had all been staged.

I leaned over the stacked bricks, adding to the lists of obstacles between where I was and where I wanted to be. I sat on the ledge, with the hope that a gust of wind would end this lonely moment. I looked down and saw a crowd of artists, trying to paint their perfect scenic canvas. Most, just calling their attempts abstract; only a few stood out as the real Salvador Dalis. I, on the other hand, didn't have my own paintbrush and as of this morning I didn't even have a canvas on which I could paint my life.

I closed my eyes and heard no sound; the world seemed to have paused around me. No construction, not even the discordant sound of constant traffic. For a split second I felt like I didn't exist; that's when I felt more alive than ever. This was one of those epiphanies; you hear great scholars and inventors constantly rub in your face in those umpteen interviews and documentaries dedicated to their fame and superiority. But my revelation wasn't to create but to destroy.

For once, I was in control of my actions—the captain of my own ship. Even though mine had sunk when it was half way across the ocean, I was still in control of the chaos that starred just me. I had the power to enhance it or to get rid of it and I had chosen the latter. I stood up. This time I didn't need a gust of wind to make me shiver; my feet started trembling with no assistance. I closed my eyes and was about to leap forward, but I couldn't. I failed at failing and I still needed another reason to end this, to end me.

This time, I turned my back so I didn't have to fall face first. I was good at turning my back on problems, so one last time wouldn't really hurt. I tried making it dramatic. I put my left foot in the air, but just before the right could join it, I heard a terrifying scream and the screams seemed to increase when a group of suited men rushed out into the restricted terrace. I stumbled in shock and fell face first, right next to a pile of bricks stacked in front of me. My heart had skipped a few beats as I tripped, so it compensated by beating faster. Inevitably, I broke into a sweat. What was I thinking? Why did I not want to complete the Rubik's cube? These questions then led me to think how I had failed yet again within the span of three minutes, failed at jumping in the right direction. I was brought out of my own thoughts immediately by loud voices on the other side of the terrace. There was the evitable panic in their voices, leading me towards them. A group of stock traders, in suits, some on the phone, the others with their hands on their heads, were leaning over the ledge, shouting and creating havoc. A similar scenario to the mayhem that had erupted in 2008 when the markets crashed.

I glanced at what had caused these shouts and way down

below I could see the minuscule figure of a man, in a suit, his body distorted and painted in a pool of his own red blood. I looked closely and it was a man much like me, who had leapt forward onto the correct side, getting rid of his paint brush and crushing his canvas. He too had a briefcase; his had more documents, it seemed, which were scattered all around the construction site he had chosen to end it all at.

I panicked and quickly ran back to my spot, picked up my briefcase and headed straight through the door I had thought I would only be walking through once. But just as I did, I was stopped by two pale faced men in suits. They questioned me about the incident, asked me what I had seen and why I hadn't stopped it. They asked me more questions than they had in the final round of my job interview, but this time I couldn't answer even one of them.

I used to love high rise buildings, now I am trapped in one. Now I hate them. I thought I could solve puzzles but it turns out I can't. Especially, if this puzzle was broken.

I was sentenced to life imprisonment for the murder of Rahul Bannerjee, vice president of the same company that had hired me for my first job, the same company that had fired me before I could begin my first job. VP Mr Bannerjee had been on the other side of the terrace trying to do the same thing I had failed to. Why? Because he too had been fired. It turns out you can't fire employees before they begin their jobs without suitable reasons. It also turns out you aren't capable of paying fourteen new employees when your company has gone bankrupt. He had been framed. The same men on the terrace who had pretended to be devastated by his death had been the money laundering scums that had caused the company to go bankrupt. They had driven Bannerjee off the ledge. They made him fire all the other new employees and before their company could be sued, they had fired him for poor execution and blamed him for the losses. Oh the irony! They had led him to the ledge but I had been charged for pushing him off it. Did I try and defend myself? Yes. But what can you do when evidence suggests that fibres from your clothing were on the clothes of the victim of suspected murder?

I had been the last person to be fired by him. Along with a three months' compensation salary; I was given a tight, sympathetic hug, which I had reciprocated with the same force but in a fit of rage. So when the investigation into his death started, it turned from a suicide case to a murder, the instant the forensics team found my suit's fibres on the front of his crushed blazer. Crushed, from the force applied by me, by my hand prints. The police didn't think twice before investigating all fourteen of us fired newcomers; with my DNA being found in a greater ratio on his body, I was the candidate they hired to become the prisoner. I was announced as the murderer while the other stock traders, the ones who had caused these excruciating events, were not even questioned once.

Now I have all the time within these four walls to solve my Rubik's cube. The fuck up is I have one with missing pieces.

Sensation

It seems like a hundred years have passed,
And I'm just sitting on my own,
Trying to sing each unwritten verse,
Hoping things could reverse,
And I know I'm late,
We don't know who made this mistake,
But this time, the blame I am willing to take,
To get over this break,
And be there now,
Far from here,
Close to near,
Near the tree that made you dear.

Near the study, where we learnt more about ourselves,
We spoke for hours, studied each other for even more,
What I'd give to rewind each moment.

I'd say I miss you but that you will always know,
It's the only emotion that keeps us connected,
I'd take this piercing sensation than ever feeling rejected.

Members Only

We were both students. We both had part-time jobs. My profession was a bit unconventional to her, hers was eccentric to many. I worked as a receptionist at the university I studied in. She laughed at the irony. 'You pay them thousands a year to earn a few hundreds an hour. Why don't you just pay them ₹10,000 a week less for your tuition?' She had a point but I wanted to be noticed. She, on the other hand, never wanted to be noticed. Her name, her names, were Dana and Disha. I knew Dana before I met Disha. She studied drama, wanting to act in musicals and take the stage at London's Queen Theatre followed by New York's Broadway.

She was gorgeous, all the way from her fake bob cut blonde wig as a disguise along with her four inch long, plastic heels on which walked an elegant five foot six inch, Dana.

If only I had been able to look a little further into the future ten hours ago and know where my steps would guide me. Then I wouldn't have gone through the anguish which led me to this agony. The butterfly sensation in the stomach we learn about as youngsters as a warning when we are bound to concentrate most of our time on someone else has a different side once this concentration goes to waste. These wasted moments from the past help in creating a sensation when all these butterflies inside our stomach die, leaving a void. Pictures soon become flashbacks and words are constant reminders of days where generosity and togetherness were not deemed selfless acts but normal.

I stood looking at a bag of clothes strewn half out of my suitcase. I wanted to curl up, lock myself in it and throw away the key. The printed airline ticket on my desk was now a mere piece of paper that had been used to scribble thoughts which we had previously shared with each other. I had had more than eight cups of black coffee overnight and I floundered, unsure whether it was the brew that was keeping me awake or the constant internal conversation. My body was jet-lagged and it guided me towards my room. I forced myself to clear the thoughts in my head and the memories that led to them. Tomorrow was supposed to be our getaway for my birthday but since today she chose to do just that; however someone else is escorting her. Her words, her action, written and sent to me through a letter wounded me like shrapnel. I was so convinced she was the sole reason for my happiness that other aspects of life seemed pointless. I stood straight faced, ignoring all the warmth life had to offer me to compensate for all that I hoped she would offer me. Anything that can drive us insane is either good or bad for us. We need to be gamblers, betting on the correct number. Love, lust, infatuation and sexual cravings are never good reasons. Nevertheless, statistics state these are the most opted for.

I felt useless only because all the hormones that had rushed in my body for years now did not cause a spike in my breathing each time I thought of her. Tired, beaten like a defeated boxer, my body ached as I ripped out pictures of us in times we had said all that which proved to be a lie now. I began tidying up my room, throwing the clutter in a box dedicated to the mistake which I had devoted my time to; it had been one-sided, where only I was loyal. My tiny room, which had been our castle when she graced it, now whispers abuses for my naivety. It was as though love had made me blind to any fault she'd make. As I read this letter, I hope the man she left me for is not conned by her false devotion. Humans can only be prepared to endure physical pain. I felt as though my bones had been shattered individually while my flesh had been burnt by a blow torch.

With all the letters in which she penned her emotions, that now seemed like ink blots staining a sheet, was an envelope which read, *'Open this when you have torn up all the pictures.'* The writing that had been scribbled on it with a pen running out of ink resembled that of a kindergarten student or an intoxicated adult. I didn't have to open this previously used, untidily taped envelope to know it was from my closest friend and critic. The contents could be a definite, *'I told you so.'* He had warned me about the reason for my despair like a psychic. Friends who don't like your girlfriend can be jealous of you or don't like her for reasons that are hidden from the blinders love puts on us. However, close friends could be a combination of both and this could be the primary reason I had ignored his sixth sense till judgement day.

'Open the letter, Mr Romeo. This one won't disappoint.'

The text message from my closest friend that filled the silent room with noise reaffirmed that men have a strange way of dealing with despair and sadness. Being harsh, upfront and acting oblivious are methods of consoling a friend and I was the victim of these methods. Keshav and I had known each other for years; we shared a friendship in which lies had no place. A storehouse of everything you need to know about me, he stood behind me to trip me for fun and hold me up when someone else tried to trip me. It was no surprise he sensed fear like a dog. Which he was in the unconventional sense and in the conventionally loyal manner, we were both loyal to each other. He gave me my space because, as he'd put it, *'It would give me enough time to ponder till I got stuck in my thoughts,'* just so he could slap me out of it. Exhausted from my internal conversations, I tore open the carefully saved envelope that had accumulated dirt from being passed around like a family heirloom. Since it was worn out and it was easier to rip apart; out of it fell a black rectangular card with sharp edges and a smaller matching version resembling a credit card.

I stood with sunken eyes staring at an invite and a membership card to India's first ever strip club. Being a 20-year-old man, my adrenaline should have pumped harder than a skydiver's but the fear of the unconventional and new kicked in quicker. I was hesitant, unable to wonder whether this was a prank being played to annoy and disturb me about something else, so I researched the details. My hometown, the capital of my country, had accepted newer business ventures and this gentlemen's club was the first of its kind. The way to mend a man's heart isn't through the sexual organs; this invite was an aphrodisiac to divert my attention. I don't know what strings Keshav had pulled but his influential family background worked wonders; it had presented me with the opportunity to a VIP room experience, whatever that entailed. As oblivious as a child speaking his first word, the words written on this invite seemed foreign to me. The black membership card had an elegant sheen, reflecting the cloudy image of my dry eyes and impassive expression. Scared because I did not know what was in store, Keshav's attempt to divert my attention to another subject was already successful. I was nervous. Skeptical about visiting a place where women were objectified, but then a profession must be respected. These women were paid to do whatever you imagined and not the other way around. These arguments bounced back and forth. My lack of knowledge and experience about strip clubs made me nervous. India had progressed from what I had read with regards to its roads before I was born, but the norm and thought process was still very conservative. I turned painful memories over in my head. My fingers ached from tearing pictures twice as many times as we had taken them and my body craved sleep. The clock had ticked twice over each hour, and it had been over 24 hours since I slept. My eyes felt like weights were pulling them to the ground to finally rest. As I lay down near the pillow, I didn't need the second one because habit stated it was hers to rest on. I threw it onto the box, a memory to be discarded. My brain slowed down towards the end from exhaustion as the invite that flashed 7 p.m. became my reason to wake up an hour before the stated time to make it on time to my VIP room experience.

I stood outside a brown, swinging door, on a cold December night, fifteen minutes before my appointment. I wasn't sure whether it sounded too formal to call it an appointment but I was certain I couldn't call it a date. The body-hugging jumper clung to my body tightly as I shivered from the cold and anxiousness. In two minds about my decision, I was nudged several times by a group of men. All of them dressed in blazers, they looked like a pack of uniformed students rushing into the doors, scanning their IDs, impatient to get a glimpse of the new attraction in the city. The media was hovering unasked and unwanted, blinding the bouncers who were standing sternly like wax figures; the media people's cameras flashed lights that could stun a deer. My feet pointed towards the door though the rest of me was too shy to enter. I needed a push from behind and that's what I got as a voice, resonating as if it was coming through a mic, addressed me.

'Not going in, Sirji? Are you a reporter as well?' He had a tall frame and glanced down as he towered over me, making me seem like a shadow in his presence.

'No, this is my first time here, I was given this.' I flaunted my invite without meaning to seem like a show-off. I watched him scan the IDs with a monitor that reinforced that technology had come a long way.

'This is everyone's first time, Sir. Even my first day, first job today. If I was you, I'd go in.' His broken English was made understandable through his eyes that were as expressive as a Bharatnatyam dancer's.

'Why is that?' I felt more comfortable standing outside despite the strobe effect from the flashing cameras.

'This place won't stay open for too long. They try and westernize the country and bring this dirt from outside. How can we learn our culture when they instill such values and lifestyles?' His question was rhetorical but he was searching for an answer. The sudden intensity in his words and lack of understanding of what was taking place behind the doors he manned spoke of the cultural barrier more than what he seemed to think it was. His words made me rebellious about my own beliefs as I chose to enter the hole filled with alcohol and high levels of testosterone. The entrance had the most absurd lighting I had encountered; the passage was dark and the corners of the walls lit. The music became louder with each step and so did my anticipation to witness what I was edging closer to. I walked into what resembled a posh nightclub with acrobatic women in the finest lingerie performing stunts I had seen in films. I was in awe of the beauty bestowed upon my eyes. The exquisiteness was from the aura that was reflected by the environment occupied by restless men and the prettiest and most charming women who spoke to these intoxicated swaying men.

There was a lot to soak in but I was not where I was supposed to be. Lost and astray, I found the only man in a suit not distracted by the women who resembled sketches in art books. I was escorted into a dimly lit purple room with a leather sofa and two leather recliners. Preoccupied by my new surroundings, my movements were still awkward and I made myself comfortable on one of the chairs, situated opposite a silver pole that shone brightly in this purple lighting. The purple chandelier on top of my head cast designs around me, hypnotizing me so I would calm down in the aromatic room. This spacious cabin had its own music adding to the relaxed environment; a piano and trumpet duet soothed my nerves, and the dark thoughts that had bothered me in the day faded away. As I began to swim in my internal monologue, someone with the gentleness and light-footedness of a ballet dancer entered the door I had been led through. She stood in a light blue satin robe that teased a hint of the lingerie she wore underneath.

'Phones and photography are not allowed here,' standing confidently, she gave instructions like a flight attendant before take-off. Her fake blonde wig was evidently a disguise but the voice that reached my ears as a balm to my nerves, tricked me into feeling as if I had been caught cheating during an exam.

'Yeah, I didn't know. I'm not taking any pictures.' My words and discomfort in the leather chair I was sitting in demonstrated that I had obviously been brooding and had yet to stop.

'Why do you seem like you've been forced here?' her voice was so confident, it reminded me of the flag bearer during my school march past; a speech so poised it could assemble a room full of soldiers with one command. We were alone in a dimly lit, purple room with a chandelier suspended three feet from the ceiling, surrounded by the scent of lavender to calm the anxiety escalating within my nervous and stiff body. She drew the cream beaded curtains close, a partition between the seating area and the door. She walked straight to me in her satin lingerie, leaning over my shoulder to increase the music that serenaded us, a catalyst to calm my nerves; they eased. The lavender scent in the room now combined with her intoxicating perfume; it filled my thoughts with images of a fresh, blooming bed of lilies. A waft of her sweet aroma created a calm environment in this room for two. Sedated in the tranquility, with my senses ensnared by her, I smiled, my eyes fixated on her.

'What's your name? I'm Dana.' Her eyes had a little child's innocence which was in contrast to her sly smile. Attributes that made the perfect recipe for disaster, ingredients I was lured into developing a taste for.

'What's your name, hun?' Now perched on my shivering knee, she stroked my uncombed hair away from my eyebrows. She repeated the simple question; I couldn't find the answer. I was trapped between comforting and uneasy thoughts. I forced my facial muscles to project another genuine smile as she glanced straight into my eyes, deep enough to know I was bluffing. I shuffled on the cherry red leather sofa which reclined due to my awkward, self-conscious movements.

I didn't have the heart to tell her that I didn't want to be there, with her resting comfortably on my lap. I sat uncomfortably numb. 'It's my birthday tomorrow and my flatmate gifted me this private room experience as a combined gift and compensation for me being stood up by my recent ex-girlfriend, who chose to cheat on me a day before I planned on taking her on a weekend trip to Mumbai.' I felt relieved speaking some of my first words since I had entered this room.

Admittedly it was more information than I'd imagine you'd reveal to a stripper who was paid ₹30,000 an hour for a private room experience. But it felt right. Something I thought I would never again feel since I had been cheated on.

'That's a long name,' she smirked as she stood up to uncork a bottle of Moët, which had been kept in an ice bucket. It was a perk included in this first time experience for a boy of twenty who was edging closer to becoming a man of twenty-one. As she stripped the seal off, she raised the wet leaf green bottle towards me. From it escaped bubbles, gushing out from the rim like a waterfall. She poured the drink into two sleek champagne glasses, thus allowing the fermented grapes to guide us through the night.

'Sorry, I'm Raghav. I wouldn't be here if it wasn't for my friend.' Her presence left me impassive on the outside whereas on the inside I was every shade of nervous.

'Why? Are you allergic to having a good time?' she stood leaning against a shiny, silver pole, which glowed brightly adding to its sheen due to the strange purple lighting in the room. I looked at her with a sense of familiarity although we had been strangers just under fifteen minutes ago. It's funny how when we meet someone for the first time, we don't know the significance they will have in our lives, whether they will be a five minute conversation or a lifetime commitment. I knew nothing about her, despite the fact that she had made me forget all the complexities that had weighed me down. I was certain, I didn't want her to be a mere conversation.

'Can I get a refund for this?' I stuttered, solely due to the influence of the alcohol in my system. I asked her my question with the utmost genuineness.

Sauntering around the room whose walls would hear all

sorts of requests, she stopped, gazing at me while swaying her body in a fetching fashion, embracing the music that swallowed my bizarre request.

I repeated it, this time over the sound of the violin and piano duet, which seemed to power her graceful moves, as if rehearsing a theatrical movement piece. 'Can I get a refund for this?'

She stopped, tilted her head to the side with a look of astonishment and confusion. She walked towards me, showcasing the effect the second glass had had on her. She leaned over my shoulder once again, this time to turn off the music. The only sound in the room was that of heavy breathing from my alcohol infused self as she sprang onto my reclining torso. My denim jeans were now covered in glitter from her bare, arched back. She whispered gently in my ear, 'Are you usually this stupid?'

I was in absolute awe of her. Mesmerized yet nervous, the two opposing emotions didn't let me respond to her. 'No, I just wondered....'

'The first man to come into the VIP room and you wonder if you can refund this private room experience,' she smirked, questioning my sanity, completely aware of my nervy stutter.

'No but I didn't pay for this...' I sat adamantly attempting to get myself out of the awkwardness I had got myself into.

'Then how about you just ask me for something that might happen?'

'How old are you?' is all I could say to hide my gracelessness in contrast to her elegance.

'Wow! You're all about the wrong questions aren't you?' She laughed, her eyes expressing a relaxed joy and unrestrained mirth, while she emptied the bottle of bubbly into my glass. 'I'm twenty-one. Anything else you'd like to know, stalker?'

'Oh, so am I. Are you from Delhi?' My repeated questions reinforced her accusation and tag for me, while I asked her more about herself as a way to defend my cluelessness.

'So, what's your surname? How old are you? Do you like sports? What kind of sports? What is your favourite colour? Is it really a colour or is it a shade? Why are you really here if you had a choice not to come? Are you glad you're here? What colour is the wall behind you? Is it a wall or is it a mirror? Are you nervous or hesitant?' her rapid fire questions matched her hurricane personality. It was evident that she had not grown out of her childhood naivety and fun as she controlled her photogenic smile, staring me straight in my dilated eyes.

'Nervous…definitely nervous,' I sipped my drink to quench my thirst for a longer conversation.

Movies teach us that love can strike more than once; philosophical purists claim real love happens only once. I feel we're lucky if it happens just once because humans aren't emotionally stable or strong enough to face those emotions several times. I definitely wasn't and yet I could sense a new episode unfolding.

I was a movie buff but little did I know, those large projectors hypnotized me into believing I could create my own version of love and fall into its trap again, that too instantly.

She sprang up, using my body as a trampoline, now standing with her soft and delicate hands on her slim waist as she enquired in an evocative tone, 'Why don't you ask for something that might happen?'

Hearing that made me immediately sit up straight, an uncontrollable force leading to my newly glittered denim jeans being soaked with champagne, adding a chill to my body which was intensified by her suggestion.

'Let me take you out to dinner?' I exclaimed my request reflexively, as if I were destined to ask her out.

'I've already had my dinner; thanks for asking though.' Slow dancing around the room which no longer welcomed anxiety and discomfort, she replied in her mellifluous voice, fully aware I intended on taking her out on my birthday.

The dimly lit space beyond this room made hazy by alcohol and attraction was filled with men in suits who were feasting their eyes on women they knew nothing about apart from their outer beauty. Men who spent tens of thousands of rupees each night hoping that the twenty minutes they invested in would pass slower than a year, if not freeze them in time. As these agile women with slender legs danced around on the spotlighted stage, no one applauded their flexibility and technique the way they really should have. All the crowd would admire was how the dancers seductively moved their torsos, completely blind to the gracefulness and beauty each individual performer exhibited, thus suggesting their inner magnificence.

'One dinner is all I'm asking you for and to make this end quicker, let's go tomorrow. Seeing that I no longer have to go to Mumbai, I have sufficient savings for a nice birthday dinner which I'd like to take you to. We don't need to meet after this; this will purely be one dinner.' When I had finished making what sounded like a plea in the form of a well-rehearsed monologue, I felt relieved yet weighed down around her, anxiously waiting and hoping she granted me the opportunity to spend a few more hours with her.

Her arched back now faced me as she had turned towards the door which I had been escorted into twenty-five unimaginable minutes ago. She reached for the circular switch board on the left of the door and switched all the lights back on, instantly making me feel momentarily awkward. I realized I might have exceeded the provided grants of this exclusive, paid nirvana. The silence in the air began to paralyse my skin like poison, making my blood as cold as the winter air. I sat uncomfortably anxious sipping on the champagne, an antiseptic for the rejection that was to follow. A whisper from across the room tickled my ears, desperate for a response, as she tittered, 'As long as you aren't conning me into a buffet.'

I had been on a few dates prior to this but this was the only one where I knew there would be only one date. I waited outside the same strip club a night later, analysing all the widely grinning men with a gleeful spark in their eyes enter the garden of lust. I wondered if any of them would ever look beyond the outer perfection to seek the inner flawlessness, as I waited in the cold, warming my hands which had had the opportunity to embrace my date.

My watch read 11.30 p.m. when the bulky, guarded brown door swung back and forth as a swarm of testosterone infused men continued to keep barging through, their IDs in their hands. Within a fraction of seconds they were made to pave the way for a woman in a hoodie, her arm draped around one side of her body, as a shield from the cold dry air.

'Hey, I'm Disha. Dana told me it's your birthday today,' the petite woman in boots and a grey hoodie winked at me. She laughed, exhaling cold vapour, revealing her familiar face which had been covered by her thick, grey hoodie.

'I take back my condition regarding the taboo on buffets, I could definitely beat them with the appetite I've worked up,' she explained. I was dumbstruck by how attractive this brown-haired lady was in her loose clothes and climbing boots. My ears fully registered her declaration; I studied her expressive movements, storing them up for tomorrow's memories.

Clad in an oversized hooded jumper, she had a striking gorgeousness that was enhanced by her lack of awareness about her beauty. Her simplicity and lack of makeup made her various qualities all the more obvious. I looked at her perfect, hour-glass figure which she had dressed as if comfort was the theme for the night. My analysis was that this simplicity added to her array of qualities.

'I'm glad to hear that because I always intended on going to a buffet, and best of all, it's open 24×7, so be ready for a long night of eating Thai food.' My immediate response was to display the confidence that had been instilled in me, due to the pent-up excitement from the night before. A significant contrast from who I had been last night.

As we walked towards the restaurant on the street corner, neither of us spoke, rehearsing our lines for the play that would follow. With only twenty minutes to midnight, the restaurant was sufficiently packed and there were no audible, awkward silences. We entered the two storey brightly lit Thai eatery that was flooded with sounds of helpless giggles from a table of women collapsing in glee. There was a lot of noise and smoke, which was contributed by men in black suits gulping beers with a lit cigar each. The restaurant seemed to be in stark contrast to the kind of food they served, the décor favouring a lounge-like atmosphere. It was filled with embroidered couches and oval coffee tables in all corners of the room. Several speakers played their part along with the alcohol, to encourage a majority of the customers to release their pent-up energy by swaying to the jazz trumpet that was occasionally inaudible due to the laughter of the wine swilling women.

Despite the crowd and the bustling environment, I felt a

sense of privacy as though locked behind the door I first saw her walk through. Disha walked like a tigress into her den, confident with each step announcing her presence. 'Hi, yeah. I got done early today as well. Yeah...the numbers should pick up soon. This concept is too new to the country; maybe on New Year's Eve...let's give it a fortnight.' I strolled around like a tourist as she spoke, looking up at who I supposed were her colleagues. Her voice reached the floor above without sounding too loud. It was all about balance and I had none, my mind drawn towards thoughts of her.

We chose to sit by the window, away from the chaotic room which was enveloped in smoke. With each word we spoke, I felt the night fading away, the skies becoming brighter with each varying shade as the moment for us to leave was approaching. Around her the pitch of my voice seemed to fluctuate, constantly indicating when I would get overly excited or nervous in her presence, my breathing pattern displaying an evident inebriation.

Moments of joy and glee in the present make memories that, in the future, bring up the exact opposite sentiments when we think of them. Yet I was willing to live every moment of my life's happiness in this one night.

I started to learn about all her idiosyncrasies and that's what made her special to me. All her micro information was stored in my brain, encapsulated by her charm, which continued to overflow during the course of the night; I didn't mind drowning in it.

'This place has changed. I used to love Khan Market before it became so...western. What kind of Thai eatery has leather sofas and jazz playing?' Her sharp knife, cut into the chicken breast on her plate to slice a thin sliver which was directed to her widely smiling mouth.

Her observations made me soak in the music that motivated my confidence.

'Some places or people will never change...some places or people will never stay the same.' She continued to cut into her meal as I let the music seep into my body.

'Why change?' I continued asking irrelevant questions despite wanting to ask those I ideally hoped to have answered.

'Because change is good.' She was evidently prepared. Her reply came less than a second after mine.

'Is it?' I attempted to match up to her speed.

'Would you rather be stuck living the old way forever? Wouldn't you like calamari and chicken breast alongside Thai curry?' She mixed the two contrasting foods to justify her point.

'Yeah, I guess....' I was like a fish being reeled in; I felt like the hook was tugging me in her direction.

Her eyebrow raised, she looked at me evidently inquiring about my differing opinion. She reassured me by asking, 'Then?'

'Change is good.' I had meant those three words. She was the change I needed and I hadn't known it till it happened.

'What do you study?' Reversing our roles to become the interviewer she asked, her expression saying she genuinely wanted to know.

'English at Stephen's. I want to be a writer. But how do you know I'm a student?'

'I think I've seen you around campus during the theatre fest... I'm also in college,' she responded realizing I was surprised that she was a student as well.

Filling in the silence at my lack of response, she continued to intrigue me. 'I'm studying drama at Ramjas. I love theatre! Do you watch any plays? I was a part of their ten-minute act. We did this performance on gender equality but funnily enough a panel of women from some NGO protested against our content and well…we were disqualified.'

'Do you want to dance? I like this song.' In truth I was oblivious to the song but her warmth and her casualness of speech made me feel like this was where I wanted to be. Where I definitely needed to be.

'I'd like you to say that when you've danced and performed for four hours at a stretch. How about we stick to talking?'

I knew she was the one for me, and I could have been one of the many for her. I insisted we dance till our legs ached; she insisted we speak till our minds were saturated. I was glad, I didn't know how to dance and I was sure my mind would never be saturated in her presence.

'What do I call you? Disha or Dana?'

'Don't call me.' Her smile at the end of that sentence was the most stunning one I had witnessed.

'What do I call you?' she reciprocated in a sardonic manner.

'More like when do you call me?' I smiled to make up for the cheap attempt at humouring her, immediately covering up with a question I should have rephrased before asking. 'What do you want to do in life? Like, as in, work?'

'I'm doing it. I'm a stripper.' Aware of my mistake, she talked over the pause. 'Later, I want to act in plays. I like movies, too, but theatre to me is the sibling that goes unnoticed…despite it being the realest form, you know. I want that to change… But, I love my job. I get to see the truest form of a man while being me and that satisfaction can't be replicated. Anyway, what do you want?' she asked, finely carving the chicken breast that lay on a plate filled with calamari. In this moment I was enveloped by her aura and the comfort she provided with each word she spoke.

'This dinner to never end,' I coughed out in response, quick enough to not let it seem prepared, as I choked on my vinegar-soaked chips.

'You could have been cheesier, you know. Why say that?' she responded with a subtle slap to my head.

'So that I have the whole night to convince you about going on another date,' I whispered; this time carefully, feeling the sting from her playful response.

She looked down with a grin that highlighted her prominent cheekbones as she let out a chuckle of appreciation at my cringeworthy effort at flirting. She replied in a melodious and somewhat hesitant voice, 'No. Eat your meal slowly; chew thirty-two times per bite. But once we go back to our respective flats… for the rest of our lives we will be a mystery to one another.' She concluded her words with a smile while I began to chew slower than before.

I remember the first time she smiled at me with utmost sincerity, her eyes lighting up like the brightest fireworks, working a heat within my body, her perfectly aligned teeth glimmering as if competing with her radiant skin and almond-brown wavy hair. I realized that very second that this smile enveloped me, that this woman now had the ability to make or destroy me.

I was terrified about what to say to her just before my eyes would no longer be taunted by her appearance. I didn't want to be abrupt nor did I want my last words to seem pre-planned, so I mustered up the courage and hugged her goodbye, whispering, 'I'll see you tomorrow at Meherchand Market for coffee, then.' After spending two hours with her, slowly nursing each morsel of our meal to delay this moment of departure, all I could come up with as my farewell was a tacky line, a statement which could almost eradicate the smallest chance of us ever possibly meeting again.

I could feel her breath tickle my ears as I completed my desperate attempt to extend this one-sided dalliance. She sniggered, 'Don't forget your membership card.'

Before this one-off dinner, I hadn't wanted to be loved again. I hadn't wanted to be anyone's first message in the morning, last call at night or mid-day thought. Love is essentially a selfish emotion; we dedicate our time to someone else but in reality we expect them to do the same for us. So love is not being selfless and giving, it's about being greedy and always wanting to receive. Real love isn't constant butterflies and melodies in your head, it's an aching pain in your gut from being anxious when she is not around you and breathing heavily when she is. A feeling I had to prepare myself to endure.

Members Only (Script)

Characters

Raghav: Final year English Literature student at St Stephen's College. 21 years of age on 16 December. He is clean shaven with unruly hair. Recently dumped by his girlfriend, Gayeti, he is skeptical about visiting the strip club due to his minimal understanding of them and conservative thought regarding stripping as a profession. Confident around his friends, he takes a short while to get accustomed to his surroundings. A gentleman around women, Raghav gets attracted to them easily. A trait that is further intensified as he is newly single.

Shikhar: 24-year-old bouncer from Haryana, currently on the second day of his first job. He is not comfortable with working as a security personnel at a strip club, due to his lack of understanding the difference between them and a brothel, which he claims are 'sins brought into India from abroad'. He is very attentive and keeps a strict frame whilst manning the entrance and at the same time jokes around with Suresh despite the heavy traffic of IDs he has to check. A patriotic Indian and BJP supporter, he is not happy with the state of affairs in the country.

Suresh (Implied character): The second bouncer outside the gentlemen's club. He is not visible to the audience but is referred to by Shikhar.

Dana/Disha: Original name Disha; stripper name Dana in order to protect her identity. A second year student of theatre at Ramjas College, she is working evening shifts at her first job in India's first ever strip club. The first from her family to attend college, she comes from a low income family. At 20 years of age, she is most confident whilst being inside the strip club where she claims to be the superior entity due to her control granted by her job over her clients. Aspiring to become an actress who can travel the world and take the stage at London's Queen Theatre followed by New York's Broadway, she is constantly imitating her movement pieces whilst at work.

When she is not working she is very protective of herself and her job, to which she doesn't take any offence. A common error made by others around her, who aren't used to the concept of strip clubs.

Keshav (Implied character): Raghav's best friend, who stays in the same student accommodation as him. He is not visible or audible to the audience but is a key part to Raghav visiting the strip club.

Gayeti (Implied character): Raghav's ex-girlfriend.

Note

'…' at the end of a line, signals an interruption.
'…' within a line signals a short pause.

Scene 1

It's 2034 on a cold December Saturday night at 11.00 p.m. in Khan Market, Delhi. Raghav, wearing a blue blazer with a crisp light pink shirt, of which the collars are buttoned to the shirt stands nervously with his hands crossed behind his back, as if in attention during a school march past. He is standing right centre stage, a few feet away from the wings, facing a brown door that swings open frequently and is manned by two bouncers. One of them, Shikhar, is visible to the audience and is accompanied by Suresh, who is not physically present for the audience to see. The entrance where Raghav is standing at is facing a road that is upstage on his right side, on which there is regular traffic. The pavement on which they are standing is filled with a stretch of restaurants with outside seating. The distance between the door on centre stage right and the right wings will be covered from centre stage to upstage with a black cloth, which will be uncovered in Scene 4. This covered portion in Scene 1 will depict the entrance and steps down to the strip club.

Raghav is clean shaven, with his hair neatly combed to the right. His dark grey jeans folded from the bottom, over his brown leather shoes, in order to add a hint of casualness to his predominantly formal attire.

He stands outside the door and is occasionally moved aside by a swarm of men who are visualized to walk past him through the door, post having their IDs checked by the two suited bouncers who stand firmly at their designated spots. The IDs are checked on each person's phone and then scanned with a device held in the bouncer's hands.

Shikhar is a well-built bouncer from Haryana, at his first job. He is intrigued by Raghav, who he sees standing outside the gate in the midst of frantic men who, like him, are dressed in formals and are rushing through the doors.

Upstage left, the curtain behind showcases a dark shadow with mild lighting on him. A man appears naked, sitting on a bed. The setting of where the naked man will be seated is a cramped university accommodation that will entail a single bed on top of which will be *present a suitcase with clothes half in and a few scattered on the bed. On the right hand side of the bed, will be a wall on which Raghav's personal pictures will be stuck, predominantly with pictures of him and Gayeti. A revolving study chair will be present towards the door, with books stacked in an unorderly fashion, near the door which will be on the extreme upstage left. The door will only be present to the audience when it is opened. The shadow image that will be observing the conversation is Raghav's mind, which will get anxious towards the end of Scene 1.*

Raghav: This is my first time over here...mein andar nahi ja raha par achha lag rahan hain yahan se... *(Hands placed behind his back, he looks up at Shikhar mid-sentence)*

Shikhar: *(Replies with his eyes on the IDs in his hand)* Yeh sabka first time hai.

Raghav: Haan...that toh it is. But I haven't gone here when I went outside India either.

Shikhar: *(Not catching on to his English completely)* Huh?

Raghav: Mein yahan kabhi abroad bhi nahi gaya...so it's my first time only.

Shikhar: Sirji...aap abroad toh gaye ho.

Raghav: *(Silent)*

A group of eight moderately intoxicated men come out of two taxis that stop on the road opposite the door. They pay the taxis and walk in between and past Raghav to enter.

Shikhar: *(Pointing amidst the crowd of men scattered in an unorderly manner to a man trying to walk into the club)* Sir, sir... haanji you, ID please?

Sir, gymkhana club ka card nahi, driving license. Haanji... Membersip card ke liye, andar jaake steps se right wale counter par. *(Gestures into the door)*

Shikhar: *(Aims the question at Raghav as the crowd of men enter)* You are reporter? Story chhaapne ke liye aaye ho kya?

Raghav: Nahi...

Shikhar: Phir, andar kyun nahi jaa rahe?

Raghav: Mein kal gaya tha...aaj bahar hi hoon.

Shikhar: Hahaha! Sir, aap bhi... Pehle kyun jhoot bola? Kya pehle din hi aapka membersip card le liya humne? Jugaad karaaun aapke liye? *(Winks at Raghav as he completes his suggestion)*

Raghav takes offense to his statement and gets defensive as he replies.

Raghav: No! I'm waiting outside. Mujhe bulaya hai bahar.

Shikhar: Chalo sahi hain. Issi bahane hamaari dosti bhi ho gayi. I am Shikhar Khatri Sirji, from Haryana.

Raghav: *(Not wanting to give away his name)* Achha.

Shikhar: Sir, ek baat bataun aapko, Suresh aur mein abhi hi discuss kar rahe *the... (Points at Suresh)*

Raghav: *(Now calmer, putting his hands in his pocket while saying it)* Bolo Khatri ji.

Shikhar: Doosra din hi hua hai is jagah ko...par yeh ek-do mahino mein hi band ho jayega.

Raghav: Aap itne bharose se kaise keh sakte ho?

Shikhar: AAP ke vajhe se hi toh.

He laughs along with Suresh while Raghav doesn't get the humour.

Raghav: Huh?

Shikhar: Haha! Arre Sir aap samjhe nahi…Bees saal pehle jab Modi ji aaye the kabza karne toh yeh Hindustan kabhi nah soch paaye ki aisi jagah Dilli mein khule…Ab Congress vaapas ah gayi hai or Dilli mein AAP. Road-woad toh saaf kara diya magar yeh gandagi vilaayat se yahan le aaye.

Raghav: India badal raha hai!

Shikhar: Kahan Sir, aap bhi mazak hi kar rahe ho.

Raghav: *(Silent)*

Shikhar: *(Points to the road, upstage)* Woh dekho, woh makaan… bahut hi aalishan hai na? Ab uske paas dekho, woh chhajje jaisa ghar koi madhumakhi bhi na jhel paaye…Woh kisi gareeb ka ghar hai. Upar upar se kisi cheez ko saaf karne se woh naya nahin banta…

Raghav: Saaf toh kar rahe hain na; bees crore aur log hain ab is desh mein. Sabki dekhbhaal kaise kargoe aap?

Shikhar: Mein nahin Sir, mein toh is hi gentlemen's club ko apni seva doonga *(Looks up at the board while reading it. The board is visible to the audience but not the letters on it)*

As he does so, the door is opened by him midway as it's pushed and he makes way by asking the other men who are waiting to enter to move aside, as a girl wearing a hood up and jeans walks outside.

Disha: *(Looks around rubbing her hands together to warm them as she looks at Raghav)* Hi, I'm Disha, Dana told me about you *(Smiles as she says that).* Happy Birthday *(She hands him a membership* *card),* you forgot this last night.

Raghav: *(Looking at the bouncer as if indicating this is who he was waiting for)* Hi, uh…ya, thank you.

Raghav: You're looking nice…

Disha: You say that as if you're surprised…

Raghav: Oh…no not like that!

Disha: Haha! Well I'm glad you like my finest dress.

Raghav: *(Smiles)*

Disha: I take back my condition regarding the taboo on buffets…I could definitely beat them with the appetite I've worked up.

Raghav: I'm glad to hear that because I always intended on going for a buffet. *(No sign of nervousness present in his voice)*

Disha: *(Laughs quietly and is interrupted mid laugh)*

Raghav: Oh and the best bit…it's 24×7, so be ready for a long night of eating Thai food.

They start to walk silently towards the restaurant which is on the corner of the street. Neither of them speak as if rehearsing lines for what is to follow.

They both walk off stage as the lighting fades from them and lights up upstage left with the curtains removed and Raghav's mind not present on the bed. The student accommodation is as it was described in Scene 1 behind the curtains but has no one in it as the lights come on.

Scene 2

Raghav is seen entering, talking on the phone and tearing pictures. This is Raghav, a day before Scene 1.

Raghav: I know, I know; but such things don't happen you know. I mean, how can I, how can it? No...Keshav I understand but I thought maybe she wasn't. I thought it was a joke of some sort. A fucking terrible joke...

He is seen taking clothes out his bags and dumping them on the bed with occasional temper looming into his actions.

Raghav: Yea, I understand...okay. No, you don't need to come over. Bro, its fine. We'll plan something for tomorrow. I've been cheated on, not shot you fool. *(Forces laughter)*

Raghav: Bro, are you standing outside the door while talking to me?

Keshav is behind the door on the other side but is not visible to the audience. Raghav walks up to the door and puts his phone down mid-conversation as it is Keshav who is there but cannot be heard. Only Raghav's side of the conversation is heard.

Raghav: What? You thought I was going to jump down or something...I live on the first floor, itna toh hum school mein taap ke karte thein *(Again tries to laugh)*...If your fat ass allowed you to that is *(Laughs genuinely)*.

Slight pause, as Keshav replies.

Raghav: Haan, fine man! Cut me some slack abhi. I'm allowed to vent at someone! I've been dumped a day before I turned 21! A DAY BEFORE 21!

Keshav gives him a membership card (The same card he is handed by Disha in the scene before) and an invite.

He looks at it and then reverts to it again with a quick response as he looks up.

Raghav: What is this?

Keshav indicates that he should open the invite as Raghav does to read the invite to the opening of India's first gentlemen's club with an already paid for VIP Room experience and a members card along with it.

Raghav: Bro, how did you manage to get this? Chori karke toh nahi laaya?

Keshav responds as Raghav waits for a few seconds.

Raghav: Trust Ishaan to have set this up man, but I'm not taking this dude. You know meri phat ti hain in cheezon se. I can't man. You go for it. This can be your return gift.

Keshav replies again.

Raghav: Man, I don't care if it's legal; but I can't go alone. This VIP treatment, membership card and all is just not me.

Keshav persuades him as he walks off. Raghav now speaks to him in a louder tone as Keshav is down the hall.

Raghav: Chal, thanks man, I'll call Ishaan abhi... If I knew you guys would be so generous I would have made Gayeti cheat on me earlier, hah! (*Sarcastically*)

He closes the door as he stares at the invitation and membership card. He puts it on the bed and walks over to the wall next to it and goes back to tearing pictures. He continues to unpack his bag. He puts it under the bed and starts looking for clothes to wear; he picks up a buttoned jumper.

Lights fade.

Scene 3

Centre stage will be accommodated by a round table with two chairs and a wine cooling basket, with a bottle of Moët champagne in it. The wine cooler will be covered by a cloth. Raghav will be seen sitting doodling on his phone, wearing a buttoned jumper, looking a bit nervous and vary of his surroundings.

A purple chandelier is on top of the stage (Implied) but the lights are focused on the chair Raghav is sitting on. A silver shiny pole is situated to the right side of the chair. The lighting is now dimmer and focused on Raghav's mind who is sitting naked on an empty bed upstage left, with the cloth covering the room which is tidier than it was in Scene 2.

This is the VIP Room of the strip club on the same day as Scene 2. A girl in a light blue satin robe with lingerie under walks in from right centre stage, which makes Raghav sit up nervously. It is Disha, now known as Dana.

Dana: Phones aren't allowed here.

Raghav clumsily puts his phone into his left pocket.

Raghav: Yea, I didn't know. I didn't mean…

Dana walks around the room, lighting candles and walks up to Raghav who is looking away and seems skeptical about sitting there.

Dana: Why do you seem like you've been forced here babe?

She leans over his shoulder to increase the volume of the music that serenades them with a violin and piano duet ('Dream of Dreams' by Brian Crain). It acts as a catalyst to calm his nerves which ease slightly, as the lavender scent of the room is now fused by her intoxicating perfume that immerses his thoughts towards a fresh bloom bed of lilies, as a waft of her sweet aroma creates a harmonic environment in this room for two.

Raghav: *(Smiles nervously)*

Dana: What's your name? I'm Dana.

Now perched on his shivering knee, she strokes his uncombed hair away from his eyebrows, as she asks him a simple question to which he can't find the answer to.

Raghav: It's my birthday tomorrow and my college friends gifted me this private room experience...

Dana: That's a long name.

She smirks as she stands up to uncork a bottle of Moët, which is immersed in an ice basket towards upstage centre. As she strips the seal off the wet bottle, she raises the leaf green bottle towards him and pours it into two sleek champagne glasses.

Raghav: Sorry, I'm Raghav. This is a gift and compensation for being stood up by my girlfriend a day before we left for our Goa getaway, a day before my birthday! *(Relieved he spoke all this out)* Otherwise I wouldn't have come here.

Dana: Why? Are you allergic to having a good time or what?

She stands leaning towards the silver pole which glows immensely, adding to its sheen due to the eccentric purple lighting in the room.

Raghav: *(Silent)*

Dana sips her drink as she enjoys the music serenading the two.

Raghav: Can I get a refund for this?

The mind behind the curtain moves anxiously whilst sitting on the bed, with each word he says.

Sauntering around the room, she moves as if imitating a theatrical movement piece eloquently, ignoring his request.

Raghav: *(Repeats; this time overpowering the duet of the violin and the piano)* Can I get a refund for this?

She stops, tilts her head to the side with a look of astonishment and confusion, as she walks towards him and leans over his shoulder once again, this time to turn off the music. The only sound the room is now embraced with is that of heavy breathing which is developed from his alcohol infused body as she sprung herself on his reclined torso.

Dana: Are you usually this stupid?

Raghav: No, I just wondered...

Dana: The first man to come into the VIP room and you wonder if you can redeem the ₹30,000 private room experience... Hmm, are you high or something?

Raghav: No but I didn't pay for this...

Dana: Then how about you just ask me for something that might happen?

Raghav, now even more nervous, starts taking large sips of his drink to calm himself.

Raghav: How old are you?

Dana: *(Laughs while pouring him another drink)* Wow! You're all about the wrong questions, aren't you?

Raghav: No, I didn't mean...

Dana: I'm 21...anything else you'd like to know mister?

Raghav: Oh, so am I. Are you from Delhi?

Dana: Are you trying to be a stalker?

Raghav: *(Laughs nervously)*

Dana: *(She asks all these questions in one breath and picks up her drink as she smiles at him)* So, what's your surname? How old are you? Do you like sports? What kind of sports? What is your favourite colour? Is it really a colour or is it a shade? Why are you really here if you had a choice not to come? Are you glad you're here? What colour is the wall behind you? Is there a wall or is it a mirror? Are you nervous or hesitant?

Raghav: Nervous...definitely nervous *(Sips... his drink; this time more confidently)*

Dana: So Raghav, why are you here? I know you said your friends forced you and all but...why are YOU here?

Raghav: Because my friends...

Dana: No, that's not why; but never mind...it's been twenty minutes and I can assure you this isn't what your friends had in mind when they sent you for a VIP experience.

Raghav: Oh...okay. What is...

Dana: I thought the questions had stopped! Haha! You're like an investigator at a crime scene! I'm going to give you one last question, make it the right one yea?

Raghav: Let me take you out for dinner?

Dana: I've already had my dinner, but nice of you to ask.

Lilting around the room which no longer welcomed anxiety and discomfort, she replies in her mellifluous voice fully aware that he intended on taking her out on his birthday.

Raghav: One dinner is all I'm asking you; and to make this end quicker, let's go tomorrow. See, I have money saved from my cancelled trip and if you don't mind, then we can go... Just one dinner; we don't have to even meet after that.

She springs up as he completes his request, using his body as a trampoline. Her arched back now facing him as she turns towards the door she entered from. She reaches for the circular light board on the left of the door and switches all the lights back on (All lights of the theatre to be turned on), instantly bringing a sense of momentary awkwardness run down Raghav's spine, as he realizes he might have exceeded the provided grants of this exclusive paid nirvana.

Dana: *(Whispers from across the room)* As long as you aren't conning me into a buffet.

Lights out.

Scene 4

The curtain covering the door centre stage right as the entrance to the strip club is now removed. On the other side of the door which was first covered, is Dana; whereas Raghav and Shikhar are standing at the entrance of the strip club. They are seen speaking in the same manner they were in Scene 1 but are inaudible to the audience. The mind will be visible as it was in Scene 1 with Raghav. On the other side Dana enters from the door centre stage right into a room that will be the common changing area with a long table opposite a mirror, with a row of chairs kept. Each stripper has a set area for their belongings.

Dana's back is facing the audience at first and she enters and sit on her chair. Her face is now only visible through the mirror reflection. She will start removing her wig which she uses as a disguise and seems skeptical in doing so as she is more comfortable in it.

She then goes behind a curtain near the table and changes into a hoodie and jeans behind it with her back still against the audience.

Dana: Yea, I'm done for tonight…What about you? *(The other voice will be implied and not audible).* Hahaha! Lucky you, I'm in tomorrow though… Yeah, it was alright. He seemed really nervous, so I got a big tip out of that. Wait, what? He really asked you that?

Dana now walks out in a hoodie and jeans with no makeup and her real image is visible to the audience for the first time. She goes and sits on her chair where she begins to wear her boots, still talking to her friend.

Dana: Yea, I could sense this one wanted to ask me for something as well. I just kept pointing to the boards on his side…hmm, how about next time we just tell them this isn't a brothel? They all seem to speak more from their eyes than their mouths… I feel like a psychic because I know what's on most of their minds when they enter…I know, anyway, I'm off now, I'll see you on Sunday. No, you girls order in, I'm off for dinner. No… not a date…Anyway, bye!

Dana's confidence and personality whilst in the club sobers as she starts to exit and meet Raghav. She starts to walk to the exit and before she can walk out, she pulls the hood over her head and pushes the door to go outside as it is opened midway by Shikhar who clears the path for her by moving aside the crowd of people.

Disha: *(Looks around rubbing her hands together to warm them as she looks at Raghav)* Hi, I'm Disha, Dana told me about you *(smiles as she says that)*. Happy Birthday *(She hands him a membership card)*, you forgot this last night.

Raghav: *(Looking at the bouncer, as if indicating this is who he was waiting for)* Hi, uh...ya, thank you.

Raghav: You're looking nice...

Disha: You say that as if you're surprised...

Raghav: Oh...no, not like that!

Disha: Haha! Well I'm glad you like my finest dress.

Raghav: *(Smiles)*

Disha: I take back my condition regarding the taboo on buffets...I could definitely beat them with the appetite I've worked up.

Raghav: I'm glad to hear that because I always intended on going for a buffet. *(No sign of nervousness present in his voice)*

Disha: *(Laughs quietly and is interrupted mid-laughter)*

Raghav: Oh and the best bit...it's 24×7, so be ready for a long night of eating Thai food.

The two of them start walking silently towards the restaurant; walking past other diners with seating filled with people enjoying the music that was mused from the close proximity of the restaurants to each other.

They exchange smiles and glances with each other, communicating thoughts without speaking until they enter the Thai diner.

The man behind the curtains is now wearing clothes and playing jazz through a trombone which is heard and it gets fainter. He then puts the trombone down and sits down as the mind. He is dressed exactly the same as Raghav.

They are now at the Thai diner they walked towards in Scene 1. It is brightly lit with yellow lighting that is overpowered with helpless giggles from a table of women collapsing with ecstasy. The noise level is high and so is the smoke, which is contributed by men in black suits gulping beers with a lit cigar each to accompany them.

The two storey restaurant contradicts the theme of their food, with their décor favouring a lounge filled with oval coffee tables and low chairs. Several speakers around the premises play their part along with the alcohol to bring the majority of the customers to relieve pent-up energy by swaying to the jazz trombone that is occasionally inaudible due to the laughter of the wine filled women.

Disha looks up and admires the two storey restaurant, which is fairly packed for 11.40 p.m.

Disha: (Looking up, talking to a colleague of hers) Hi, yeah, I got done early today as well. I thought you'd be ordering in with the others... No, he's a friend, and this isn't business, haha! Yeah...the numbers should pick up soon. This concept is too new in the country; maybe on New Year's Eve...Let's give it a fortnight.

Raghav walks awkwardly taking short steps, looking around the ambience and restaurant.

Disha: This place has changed. I used to love Khan Market before they became so…western. What kind of Thai diner has leather sofas and jazz playing?

Raghav: Yeah, let's sit there by the window.

They are now seated with plates filled with food. Dana's food is more scattered on her plate whilst Raghav's is finely placed.

Disha: How's your birthday going? More importantly, where's the cake?

Raghav: I thought you were bringing it *(Laughs softly)*. I haven't cut one yet.

Disha: *(She speaks as she puts a bite of chicken in her mouth)* This place will definitely have loads…

Raghav: Yeah, what kind of place keeps chicken breast, calamari and Thai curry on the same table…

Disha: A buffet. *(Takes a bite of calamari, which is immersed around a chicken breast)*

Raghav: I guess.

Disha: *(Observing the people around them)* Some places or people will never change…some places or people will never stay the same.

Raghav: Why change?

Disha: Because change is good.

Raghav: Is it?

Disha: Would you rather be stuck living in the old ways forever or wouldn't you like calamari and chicken breast alongside Thai curry at the same time…

Raghav: Yea, I guess...

Disha: Then?

Raghav: Change is good.

Dana scoops up a bite of chicken and calamari at the same time as she indicates and smiles at Raghav, reinstating his previous claim.

Disha: What do you study?

Raghav: English at Stephen's. I want to be a writer. But how do you know I'm a student?

He prepares a bite as he inquires.

Disha: I think I've seen you around campus during the theatre fest...

Raghav: Oh, really! How come you were there?

Disha: I'm also in college.

Raghav: *(Doesn't respond but looks up as he is taking a bite, and nods)*

Disha: I'm studying drama at Ramjas. I love theatre! Do you watch any plays? I was a part of their ten minutes act. We did this performance on gender equality but funnily enough the panel of women from some NGO protested against our content and well...we were disqualified.

Raghav: No, I was only there with my girlfriend.

Disha: Oh, I was the...

Raghav: I mean ex.

Time passes by and they are now talking loudly and the restaurant is emptier, however, this is implied and they are inaudible. There is a sense of comfort in their expressions as they have develop a further understanding of each other.

The mind then comes from behind the curtains dressed exactly like Raghav and pulls up a chair and sits in between them and speaks while they continue to mime a conversation.

Mind: I started to learn about all her idiosyncrasies and that's what made her special to me. All her micro information stored in my brain that was encapsulated by her charm, which continued to overflow during the course of the night and I didn't mind drowning in it.

'Pencil Full of Lead' by Paolo Nutini plays faintly in the background.

Raghav: Do you want to dance? I like this song.

Disha: When you've danced for four hours at a stretch, I'd like you to say that. How about we stick to talking?

Raghav: *(Imitates the drums with his hands and moves his feet to the music)* So what do I call you? Disha or Dana?

Disha: You don't call me. *(She smiles as she completes her sentence)*

Raghav: So Disha, then.

Disha: What do I call you?

Raghav: More like when do you call me? *(He laughs)*

Disha: There's enough cheese on my plate...I don't need more from you...*(She grins at him)*

The music fades and mutes.

Raghav: Alright, what do you want to do in life; like as in work?

Disha: I'm doing it, I'm a stripper.

Raghav: *(Silent, taken aback by her style of response)*

Disha: Later, I want to act in plays. I like movies, too, but theatre to me is the sibling that goes unnoticed...despite its realest form, you know. I want that to change... But, I love my job. I get to see the truest form of a man...while being me, and that satisfaction can't be replicated anywhere else. Anyway, what do you want?

Raghav: *(Responds promptly as he leans over the middle of the table)* This dinner to never end.

Disha: You could have been cheesier, you know. Why say that?

She gives him a subtle slap across his head.

Raghav: *(Whispers as he feels the sting of the slap)* So that I have the whole night to convince you for another date?

Disha: *(She looks down, with a grin. She lets out a chuckle of appreciation to his cringe flirtatious effort somewhat hesitantly)* No, eat your meal slowly. Chew all thirty-two times per bite if you have to; but when we go back to our respective homes...for the rest of our lives will be a mystery to one another.

They get up to leave as they are done.

Raghav's cutlery is placed finely to indicate he has finished his meal, whilst Disha's fork and knife are upside down.

Raghav's mind is still sitting in the middle.

Raghav: I'll see you tomorrow for coffee at Starbucks near campus then? *(Raghav and Disha pause as though the words from his mouth are yet to reach her)*

Mind: *(Slightly annoyed and disappointed)* After spending two hours with her, slowly nursing each morsel of our meal to delay this moment of departure, all I could construct as my bid to farewell was a tacky line...

Disha: Don't forget your membership card. *(Hugs him as she says that and walks off stage from the left as Raghav walks off from the right).*

Lights now focus only on the mind.

Mind: Prior to this one-off dinner, I didn't want to be loved again. I didn't want to be anyone's first message in the morning, last call at night or mid-day thoughts. Love is essentially a selfish emotion, we dedicate our time to someone else but in reality we expect them to do the same for us. So love is not being selfless and giving, it's about being greedy and always wanting to get. Real love isn't constant butterflies and melodies in your head. It's an aching pain in your gut from being anxious when she is not around you and a feeling of heavy breathing when she is. A sensation, I had to prepare myself to endure.

Lights out.

Seconds Turn into Minutes

Seconds turn into minutes,
Days turn to decades.
Wounds heal but the scars remain.
The memories stick but time never really waits.
The questions multiply,
The answers remain the same,
We constantly live our lives hoping to please another,
And they still argue that life isn't a game!

I knock on this door,
Push while it says pull,
Quit before I start,
Smile when I shout on the inside,
Shout while I want to play outside,
Punch the wall,
When it's the man in the mirror who should be punched.
Want the world to read my thoughts on paper,
While I can't seem to write them myself.

Seconds turn to years, thoughts turn to yearns,
As I lie here, lying to myself,
Saying this is the finish line.

I seek as I hide, run from where I reside,
And I tell myself this is how it's meant to be,
When I don't even know what 'this' really is.

Puzzle

I'm just lost in this big puzzle,
Trying to find my way out,
Without getting into a scuffle,
And I bang my knee on the edge,
From where I made this pledge.
Have I gone so far, to come right back,
Or have I just been sitting all along in this trap?

I look into the mirror and see myself smiling.
This can't be a mirror, because all I've been doing is whining.
And I've just been trapped in this complicated maze,
Sleeping through my nights and dreaming through the days.
And I look outside and see,
All there is for me.
And I break free from here,
To be where I should be.
Because this puzzle isn't going to solve itself,
This maze isn't going to go that well,
If I keep sitting here on the edge.

Obstacle

This world is a casino,
And we're all gamblers placing our bets.
Planning ahead,
Making plans we haven't made before,
Looking forward to opportunities,
That aren't guaranteed to be in store.

We make our plans,
Keeping in mind our friends and family.
Painting a picture in our head,
Smiling to ourselves about the times that are yet to be.

But gamblers don't always win,
At times the roll of the dice doesn't go our way.
Suddenly from being on a planned route,
We find ourselves lost and astray.

Whose fault is it?
Usually ours for doing something a second too quick,
Or a tad too slow.
But whose fault is it,
When you're taking all the right measures but suddenly,
You're in the midst of a big blow?

It's true then, the only certainty is uncertainty.
Does it make sense to plan ahead?

Painted Red

*H*e didn't know it but he deserved this and I made sure I whispered it in his ear as I held his head against my bloodied hands.

I carved an apology into his back; it was not from myself, it was on his behalf of the trauma he had caused while he could still have been of help. I smiled looking up at the sun that shone brightly, radiating rays that caused the red river on his back to seem even more vibrant. His body was laid out on the floor like a dismantled mannequin, drowning, stained in the congealing blood as I heard the sounds of the sirens becoming more and more audible to my ears.

I adjusted my crouched position and knelt on the thick pool of blood which formed a red carpet for my inevitable act. I stared at his ghoulish condition, with a feeling of satisfaction and an air of achievement; it was intensified by the smell of blood which was like the odour in a slaughter house. I felt a heat within my body rush through my pulsating veins as the adrenaline flowed, making me feel like I was on a roller coaster. My eyes that had been burning with rage only ten minutes ago, when this alley had witnessed one man's time run out, were still as red as the blood that painted the road. I arched my back to stare at the skies which were also witnesses to an act that had been a foreseeable consequence of my brother's murderer.

'Can somebody please help me? Please!' I shouted in panic, frantically sprinting into a brightly lit white room. My panic was intensified by the desperate gasps of breath my 7-year-old brother took as he lay like jelly in my arms.

'I need a doctor to save my brother immediately!' My body was in a state of shock. The tears wouldn't stream down my face. I was assisted by three men in surgical masks and scrubs, who rushed my brother into a room filled with surgical equipment and beeping monitors. If I had only known then that that moment was the last time I would be carrying my brother, I would have tried and bribed him not to leave with yet another football; he had loved to kick footballs.

I was as helpless as a lamb in a slaughterhouse, shivering with disbelief at the test I was being made to endure. With each blink of the eye I remembered the seven years I had spent with my little mirror image, as though it was a sign that from now on I would have to walk alone. I waited outside the room which had a lit red bulb on top of the entrance. I could vaguely hear the masked and gowned men discuss the fate of my brother amongst themselves.

'We'll need to conduct a surgery immediately. He is bleeding profusely near the external jugular and his oxygen supply will be drastically cut if we don't close the cavity caused by the bullet. Can someone call Dr Chopra immediately, please?!' I heard a stern voice, in which hints of fear were audible, say. A team followed him out of the door which was left ajar. A burning sensation within my stomach caused me to reflexively throw up by the side of the door in order to get rid of the pent-up anxiety.

I wiped my pale face with hands that were covered with the dried blood of the boy I had vowed to guard. I burst out crying to the gods, pleading they wouldn't open their doors to him.

'We'll need to wait for the police to register a case of attempted murder before we can operate on him,' a middle-aged man with short hair interrupted the group of doctors as he threw his used latex gloves into the bin.

'But Doc, the boy only has a few more minutes unless we conduct the surgery right away!' Proclaimed a junior practitioner in extreme sorrow coated with anguish, setting the tone for his argument.

'This is the hospital's policy and if you want to fuck with that and put your job on the line, why don't you go use your knowledge to be a saviour?!' As soon as he had finished mocking his subordinate, I launched myself at him. My rage had been ignited by this response from the one man whom I had thought would be able to shield my brother from his pain. 'Why?!' is all I could scream, my body too exhausted. Four sets of hands pushed me against the wall to pacify me. I choked on my words; my mind was filled with a succession of terrible outcomes, each worse than the next. My eyes were as veined and bloody as the back of a boxer's fist but the look I gave the doctors was unwavering, as was my determination to save my brother's life.

The hospital corridors, where the screams were coming from, were narrow and stuffy; the walls perpetually seeming to cave in and crush those in between them. The hallways were crammed with patients lying on their backs, waiting to be tended to while they stared at the bright fluorescent tubes that flickered as though on their last legs.

As an attempt to build up my courage, I looked into the brightly lit room when our eyes met. He was lying on his back, a pool of blood drowning the life out of him. There was a fear and terror of the inevitable around the white rimmed bulge of his eyes; I felt the coldness of it deep in my chest. I could hear his plea despite his quiet desperate gestures, as if they were exaggerated imitations of silent film actors. I felt helpless because all I could do was cry for mercy and be a mere spectator. Helpless, fearful, I could do nothing else.

I watched my brother gasp, his last few attempts to live, his chest pumping up and down, as his grey face collapsed on the left, dislodging the nasal oxygen prongs that had failed to do their job.

I tried finding meaning in this loss. I strained my eyes in desperation to open them to finally escape from the nightmare. I kept looking at the skies, waiting to hear an answer or a reason for why my brother had to be in the middle of a brawl he wouldn't have known the slightest thing about. Each question in my head was answered by another question. It burdened me, continuously driving me towards the breaking point. Fate plays its part, paving ways for some. However, it destroyed my path, leaving me feeling homeless and astray.

I stood in the middle of the busy hallways filled with echoed, muffled, angry and very rarely complacent voices. But the most terrifying voices were those that were inside the mind of the defeated. Cold, howling winds started to swirl within me, wrapping tentacles so tightly around my shattered heart that it almost stopped beating. There was no emotion left on my face by the void that was filling me from my brother's loss. I shivered with pain, emotionally bankrupt, an acidic pain in my gut conning me to believe the last few minutes had been a lie.

A spark of rage, that had been afire within my battered mind, instigated actions that would be the remedy to the eternal, everlasting pain. A scalpel from the operating theatre in my hand, I walked out of the door, following the voice of the man who had denied my brother a chance to live with the same tool that would've given my brother a new lease on life.

The doctor was standing with his cheeks sucked in,

as he exhaled the smoke from a cigarette in the lane three neighbourhoods away from where I had been sprinting with the false hope that this visit to the hospital would be merely to stitch up another playground wound that my accident-prone soldier had picked up.

I knew he had been late to save my brother as the stubbled surgeon took one last drag of the cigarette that sucked the life out of his lungs. I made sure to be there for his last few helpless minutes, while he gasped for air, just as he had been a spectator to my helpless brother's death.

No words were exchanged between the two of us, as I walked up and inserted the surgical blade into the middle of his neck, my left arm preventing him from squealing, so we could share a few more moments alone in the alley that was smaller than the narrow hallways between the walls of which my brother lay beaten.

A spite pricked my heart as I watched him gasp like my brother had, desperate for a few more tastes of fresh air to feed the hunger in his lungs. I felt cruel yet victorious because I had forgotten the difference between moral and immoral the second I had lost the only aspect of my life that had felt right.

I watched the doctor turn to look me in the eye. He was staring upwards with a face suffused with fear and foolish hope. 'We'll have to wait for the police before we can treat you,' I whispered the last words his ears could process. I was close enough to feel the stuttering breath from his wide nostrils hit my shoulder.

Life doles out tricks in the funniest ways. As children, Abhimanyu and I were both taught that life is a marathon, not a sprint, so we should pace ourselves. No one told us about all the sudden obstacles that trip us just so death could have the last laugh. What had my brother done wrong to deserve a life so short that the painful moments leading to his death seemed a lifetime longer?

Lie the Truth

It's a blank page as I begin to write,
I use the eraser more than the ink,
And these words have no respite.

I try and find the key,
Because these words seem locked inside.
I look for a map now,
These words are lost somehow.

When will you write another?
What are your plans for what lies ahead?
What's it going to be about?
I think I'll just shout forever instead.

Frustration looms,
It seems to live inside me the most,
Is it my friend or foe?

Sadness makes an appearance,
And tells me to cry,
I start to close my eyes,
Wait for those toxins to pour out,
And pretend everything will be solved as I lie.

I'll write till the ink dries out,
I'll edit till right words come alive,

I'll shout till the melody turns to magic,
I'll do all I can, so nothing is ever tragic.

I find the answers,
At least I pretend to,
If I can lie to myself about feeling glum,
I can fake happiness, till I have everything that I want done.

The Dark Side of Light

I sit here in silence,
With a voice shouting inside,
I lie here in broad daylight,
With nothing but darkness in sight.

I curl my fists that are full of rage,
And punch them into this imaginary wall,
I curl up on the inside,
Hoping I won't fall.

A thousand landmines in sight,
Yet none of them choose to go off,
Taunting me with tiny explosions as if the trailer,
I start to choke, with no sight of an inhaler.

I lie here lying to myself,
That these are in fact flowers planted to bloom,
I seek the light in the dark,
As useful as trying to use water to light a spark.

I look up
And plead,
For these years to have been just a nightmare,
I feel a drop of rain fall from the bright skies,
I smile, I laugh, anything to disguise these cries.

I look up,
And open my arms,
To whom I have pleaded once too often,
Lied about being a better me,
Each passing second makes me shiver,
Even the strongest voice in me starts to quiver.
As I lie asleep with my eyes wide open.

Airport Encounter

*H*e was right here. We had never met before yet he seemed very pleased to offer me his table, even though he hadn't finished eating and appeared to be in the middle of writing, as well.

We spoke for just over fifteen seconds and I sensed familiarity between the two of us. His voice, however, never wavered. He was as calm as a monk when he spoke, very rarely making eye contact, his hands pressing hard into the paper. His concentration and intricate writing made him seem like a tattoo artist at work. In a place crowded enough to be called a country, this airport was the tunnel that spat us out into the places we wanted to drown in. However, his frown-free reaction to each word conned me.

A sea of faces rushed across wide, structured halls that resembled cramped aisles as a swarm of jet-lagged travellers walked into and around each other. Men and women in suits rushed to gates leading to places away from where they eventually wanted to be. Children were holding toys as though they were loved ones during the long journey to places that would seem exactly the same to them as the places they had left. Pilots, air hostesses and stewards walked like an entourage, working their facial muscles to smile, spending more time off their feet than on the ground, constantly calling a new place home.

Unlike the hospital smell that made visitors feel like patients causing a wave of monotonous thoughts in their mind, this airport surrounded by taxis that defy gravity is filled with a mix of various scents. Rising from the expensive lounges, the flowery and musky smells of overpriced perfumes fused with sweat and perspiration from nervous thoughts of weary travellers.

Some walked in a line with faces like expressionless robots, while those excited ran and moved with the eagerness of children waiting to meet Santa.

Despite numerous distractions adding to the roller coaster theme of this eccentric place, I looked at his coffee which had become much lighter than it would have if he had chosen to add milk. The ice melted but this mixture couldn't faze his concentration. It caused mine to stay firm and be intrigued about what words the pile of branded tissues from the coffee house were being decorated with.

My eyes burnt from the wide eyed concentration as his creativity inked the recycled paper. My jet-lag sucked the energy out of me, making me incapable of starting a simple conversation. He started to write quicker, his hands moving like a guitarist's during a rock solo; his hands were like a musician's while his brain was orchestrating the symphonies like the conductor. As his hands began to slow down, I began to come up with thoughts and stories.

A discordant commotion was caused by impatient travellers as an announcement screamed that one flight was being delayed and the boarding for another had begun. Hypnotized by this electronic update there were opposing responses from the respective travellers leading to an increase in a clash of these partially awake bodies. *'Change of departure gate for AA flight 11 on 11 September to Los Angeles due to cancellation...'* The echo from the announcement resulted in the only swift movement I had seen him make since he had offered to share his table. He took his last bite of croissant, wiping his face as the remaining crumbs fell on his plate.

We got talking. I asked him what he did, and he told me he was a writer. I asked him what he was writing; he told me he was writing a story about a man.

He didn't elaborate any further and excused himself as he had to board his flight. Just before he left, I asked him what his future plans were. He simply replied, 'They are still to be written.'

He left just as he said that, leaving behind his pen which had run out of ink.

I'll Be There One Day

It's just another mile,
It's just another step,
It's just another moment to wait,
Before you go ahead.

I'll be there one day.

I'm just one more heartbeat away,
I'm just a few metres ahead,
I keep you waiting every day,
I'll be there one day, she said.

One Glance

There's no connection in this section,
We're sitting opposite one another,
And heading to the same direction,
I accentuate each glance as I look away,
In reality envisioning a misleading amour,
While her cinnamon brown eyes take no notice of me.

A reflection never looked so pretty,
One glance never felt so good,
Never thought I'd remember her face till now,
Don't know if she thought I would.

One smile never said so much,
Those seconds still feel enough,
It's been a while since that glance,
But I can still feel the rush.

One glance never felt so thorough,
I saw you then and I hoped I'd see you tomorrow,
But one smile was all that was written for me and you,
So I'll sit in the same seat again,
Anticipating some day that your reflection comes through.

One-sided

*L*ove is a drug we all want but fear injecting because once it's in you, it makes you powerless and takes control of your actions and then you are constantly afraid of losing it. Like a pendulum, once this chemical is discharged, it oscillates back and forth causing feelings of heat in the gut, each time you fixate on the catalyst to this everlasting sensation. A feeling that makes your heart melt each time you see, hear, smell or think of her. All of your surroundings remind you of her. When else would you stare at a pile of autumn leaves and think of her using it as a pillow? Why would you develop fondness for anything green? All for that feeling, that unifies and separates some; it did both, unified and separated us.

I don't understand the concept of love at first sight. We often get confused, finding it hard to distinguish between love and lust. To me they both play a part, complementing each other; but at the same time they are very different. Yet, I find it impossible to understand the exact moment in a person's life when they realize they no longer want to use their headspace to think of themselves but to constantly think of her, the person who was once a stranger. I wonder if there is a time tuned into our bodies when we begin to emit this feeling of love, like a specific time for a perfect sunset.

Her eyes were as green as the morning grass, followed by a nose which seemed to have been crafted by the finest sculptors. The length and curvature of either nostril were perfectly placed, highlighting her elegance. To complete the perfect canvas were her cherry coloured, upturned lips, which forever gleamed.

The first moment is usually the most memorable, a time we compare all other instances to, one that forever stays in our memory, one that no one can take away from us. I remember like it was yesterday, the two of us sat adjacent to each other, our backs to a tree, with branches long and strong enough to cradle us. We were hiding from the sun in the shade, embracing each other's company, when all I wanted to do was to embrace her. For over an hour, we talked, argued about beliefs we conveniently chose to defend just so we could get mad at each other, in order to make up after. We both saw what lay ahead; so lost in the moment, I would only realize that I was still breathing when she caught me gazing at her soft lips, which she would every so often bite with her teeth, flawless, with long canines adding character to each of her wide mouthed smiles. I did not know much about her nor of the moment we shared, but I knew she was the kind of person who would never be caught in an awkward silence. A woman so perfect, she could make me forget each and every one of my imperfections. I wanted to lean in and caress her long wavy tresses that cascaded down to her shoulders in shades of chestnut brown that were illuminated individually by the thin rays of the sun. The sun occasionally managed to sneak beyond the bouquet of leaves above our head, just so it too could be soothed by her beauty. She spoke to me about poems and music, while I nodded, pretending to be an expert in the arts; in reality nodding with appreciation at the piece of art that was leaning against a pile of dried leaves. I knew almost nothing of what she said, admiring how she would say it with intimacy and detail, punctuating significant terms with gestures of her long, thin fingers. I gazed admiringly at each movement. She would constantly pause and turn towards me for a reply and I nodded, straight faced, a defence for my relentless stares of adoration.

Nature too appreciated this cinematic scene, encouraging us with cool gusts of wind, leaving hints of the winter that was soon approaching. With each gentle breeze I pretended I was being pushed towards her, only to be nudged back to my side, reaffirming that we shared the same intentions. Our long drawn out sentences were like foreplay, unnecessary yet essential in the moments that were to follow.

In the middle of our debates, as we got to know one another's preferences, we found ourselves sitting under a navy blue sky with the shining moon the only light—like our personal lamp during this rendezvous. Deep stares; we looked into each other's eyes with no sign of discomfort, no glimmer of uneasiness. I got lost in the honey coloured irises that surrounded her pupils.

The sound of leaves being scattered and rustling by the wind, the only other sweet sound was that which fell from her gentle lips, soon to be pressed against mine as they craved the touch of hers. The moments right before our lips touched, warm from all the conversation that led to this perfect moment were a blur, as if I was in a trance. The swirling of the leaves must have whispered to the two of us to finally delve further into each other at the same time. I found myself mid-conversation with nearly all the wind knocked out of my lungs as our tongues dipped, searching for the depths of each other's mouths. Even the cold winds couldn't stop the warmth rising from our bodies, trembling from the rush of warm and cold waves that ran along our spines, acting like electricity in the intensity of the moment. My hands slowly moved their way up her curved back, as I grasped her head firmly, moving it closer to mine.

She moaned as we pulled back, gasping for a moment of fresh air. She pushed me yet again in her playful mood, using the grass and honey coloured leaves as a bed to re-enact the very first moment we had ached to relive.

The kiss that had come out of nowhere was something both of us had foreseen from the very start. Yet as we hesitantly pulled back, we smiled at one another, our lips now moist. We continued lying on the grass not uttering a word; reliving the past few minutes in our heads. In the silence, that was only interrupted by our heavy breathing, as our hearts pounded twice as fast, we were disturbed by the vibration of her phone when she stood up to leave. 'Shiv is here to pick me up; I forgot we were going for dinner. I'll see you soon,' is all I heard her say in her melodious voice that serenaded me. It had a depth to it from all the choir practice. She put her phone in her pocket, walking back alone along the path where we had both come from.

All I knew was every inch of me was saturated with love, while she walked away, adjusting her pleated skirt and retying her now messy hair. I sat still on the pile of leaves we had used as a mattress to enact what had turned out to be mere lust on her part. There was a smile on my face, accompanied by an unfamiliar, uncomfortable acidic pain in my stomach, knowing that she was walking further away from me. I was uncertain about whether we would relive this shared moment. Certain, I would make sure to relive many more with her again.

Darkness in the Light

Wandering in the dark in search of the light,
Hiding in the open, seeking shelter,
Generating friction to create warmth,
While the cold heart beats irregularly like a drum.

Feet stomp pretending to walk ahead,
Although darkness never offered a path,
And yet our footsteps imbedded within,
Misleading wanderers to walk through the road not taken.

Trust Fall

He was oblivious about where to go,
Yet they create every route,
Never letting him fall,
Always being there like a parachute.

Complementing each other like a fork would a knife,
Together they teach him not only how to make a living,
But also how to make a life.

A shadow that stays with him past the shift of the sun,
Forever catapulting him forward,
Reassuring him of triumph,
Even before the journey has begun.

Like a battery in a device,
Or simply bread with butter to be precise,
They are a duo that can make anything suffice.

The trampoline to his ambitions,
For all that he can do,
They are the real technicians.

Now they create several routes,
In the process of his indecisiveness,
They make all the scattered thoughts seem clean,
Despite all of his mess.

But wherever this route goes,
He will choose the destination despite his destiny,
It'll be right in between them where he can sense no clutter,
Where there is no indecisiveness,
Where he is nothing else but me.

Greatest Feat

There were screams, there was agony,
I'd been here before,
But this time it meant so much more to me.

I'd practiced this for years,
Used the same tools,
Witnessed the bloodshed,
But this time it had me in tears.

The excessive perspiration blurred my vision,
But I started to see even more clearly,
Perhaps because this pain witnessed,
Was to her, who is so dear?

I often had my team to assist,
But this moment could no longer resist,
And I had to execute this act on my own as one,
I can't wait for tomorrow,
To narrate to him, his birth,
The arrival of my son.

Slam Dunk

'*Dad*, when will I be able to slam dunk the ball into the net like you do?' she asked in her angelic voice, stretching her arms as high as she could, holding a ball that was thrice the size of her pretty face.

'Whenever you want, muffin!' I replied as I lifted her in my arms high enough for her to make the shot she had yearned and pleaded for, only a few seconds ago. Her pet name suited her because she too was full of surprises and was the sweetest and most caring being on the planet. As I lifted her closer to the heavens from where the angels had blessed me with her, I was the safest I would ever be. I grasped her gently yet firmly under her petite and petal soft arms; she tensed trying to use all the force she had accumulated at 3 years old to achieve her first slam dunk.

I sit here fifteen minutes prior to our meeting, looking around the café filled with conversations brewing alongside the aroma of Colombian beans. I pick up a newspaper lying near the stand on my right to absorb my daily quota of news for discussions with my peers. However, all I can imagine is an image I know well enough but only due to a few pictures, shown to me by the person I love the most. My eyes read the headlines while my brain rehearses questions and conversations that I tutor my mouth to say.

I am nervous, enough that my body feels numb overcoming the shivers, making me remember the last time my nerves had taken full control of my body. Twenty-five years and thirty-seven days ago when I first held her in my arms, nervous, not because I was scared of being a good father but anxious because that moment had been so perfect. I had wanted to make sure each moment to follow was going to be as cinematic and picture-perfect as well.

Ever since 18 February 1990, I have become a sculptor aiming for perfection, an engineer paving the perfect path, a soldier guarding his most precious possession, a father who found the complete meaning of his existence.

I look at the clock in front of me, adjacent to the door through which will come a presence I anticipate will create an aura similar to that of the gods. The second hand continues to shift, now seeming like it is moving slower than the hour hand. I have been seated here for three minutes and the air-conditioning cannot cool my brain which is thinking fast enough to make my forehead sweat.

I look down at my hands which are coloured by a fresh drop of blood from my peeled finger nail, paying the price as a stress ball during this moment.

The background music serenading us is an orchestra in a soft, feminine voice, bringing up past incidents that brought us all here, together. My mind wanders, having thoughts it is always greedy for. In a trance, nodding along to past conversations as my mind rewinds, I turn the pages to find myself smiling at a Sudoku puzzle, with numbers jumbled like my anticipation and nerves, while I sit alongside my happy thoughts medicating my anxiousness.

'I'll never be pretty, dad; I'll never get a boyfriend or go on a date, which means you'll never have to question him,' she had whispered with tears rolling down her face. The tears fell on her cheeks which tensed each time she smiled, slurring the last statement. She lay horizontal, held down by her inability to move, looking up at the ceiling filled with cards that read, 'Get well soon.' Balloons floated about like clouds in the sky. Her muttered words reassured me of her bravery, like that of the most courageous gladiator. She spoke to stop my eyes from moistening as the doctor told us that my soldier would no longer be able to turn her neck the way she could before her trampoline accident. My back was resting against the wall, adjacent to the hospital bed that she had been lying on for over thirty-six hours. I walked towards her and kissed her forehead from behind. I gathered the courage to hold back my tears, to tell her that she was the most beautiful girl anyone would and had laid eyes on. If I had been stronger, I would have told her what I had really meant was that flowers bloomed when they saw her face, she added brightness to the sun, the moon followed her wherever she went just to catch a glimpse of her beauty. But then I hoped that in time she would see all of this.

I made sure to never make her feel inadequate about her physical disability. By no means did I want her to miss turning her neck; I needed everything she wanted to be waiting in front of her. Except for the kiss I'd give the back of her head, to let her know I was always there for her, from that day on, till my last kiss on her forehead.

Despite all the reminiscing and conversations with myself, my throat dries up signifying that my nerves have overwhelmed my state of outward calm.

I readjust my position by leaning back informally in the chair, attempting to fool myself into believing that I am composed and prepared for the next chapter in my life. Nothing around me could act as a distraction, not even the cause of the sole reason for this anxiety. My ears register the sound of each passing second.

With five minutes left, I close my eyes preparing to soothe my overworked mind. I think back to a text I had received eight years ago which acts like morphine to my nerves. *'Dad, our prom just ended and Arjun asked me out to dinner tomorrow. I know you wouldn't mind if I go but I'm going to reject the offer. So can we go get pizza instead? I know you're going to insist I go on this date but please don't. I have very high expectations of what a man should be and if he has a fraction of your character would I ditch you. I love you dad (no, I'm not drunk texting you) and I want you to know that although I will move out one day, I will make sure it's not just because the man is the ideal person for me but because he is as perfect a father as you have been to me.'*

My eyes are now moist from remembering the message. I have memorized it like a script in my head. I find courage inside me. I know I won't always be there for her but as long as I am, I will make sure I am there to hold and pick her up when she falls while reaching for the stars. Ever since her light blue eyes opened to admire the world envious of her beauty, I made sure to be the perfect man, as I was fortunate to be the first one she got to be around.

Now I sit up straight, confidently folding the paper away and keeping it on the side of the table, eagerly waiting to meet her fiancé.

Comfort Zone

I go back to where I am most comfortable,
Back to the warmth to become sober and stable,
Like a gypsy with no destination,
I call each place home as it's sketched into my imagination.

My hands stop shivering as I hold this familiar tool,
To speak those silent thoughts all these times had gifted me.
Away from the past I sprain my neck looking back,
Unable to see.

I smile with nostalgia,
And a sigh of relief that the future is closer,
Than the memories of yesterday,
These days should stay coloured for eternity,
As I edge closer to grey.

A sense of familiarity seeps in like a sponge,
Reiterating with each word what I plan on doing,
And what is done,
Each syllable resonates a day that is now fully lived,
As I recreate them on this bank of thoughts.

Bringing back her smile that lit up the darkest days,
Those scared shrieks from childhood,
That keep these thoughts ablaze.
Those winter mornings,

That are as faint as the fog that hid our smiles.
Those rainy summers when we were in separate countries,
With our emotions being forced to subside.

I come to where I love being on my own,
Letting the ink write out past mistakes,
That make sense now,
As I sit in my comfort zone.

The Little Things

Time ticks on, the present soon becomes the past,
We try and live for the future,
Forgetting the small things in life,
As though they don't even last.

This isn't just about a moment,
That took a few seconds before it was gone,
These are the privileges and people,
We take for granted as our lives move along.

We take for granted what we have because it's already ours,
We're an unreasonably greedy race,
We'll want more, even if we own the stars.

Imperfection

Even brand new items might have a scratch,
We all have memories we can't erase,
We all have a few sins we wished we hadn't committed,
We all have days we hope we could re-sit.

But we all know one fact and that is for sure,
That the past is a permanent address,
And the future is just past the next door.

Yes, we all have our grazes,
Surely, we've all committed a sin,
But we need to move forward,
Instead of living within.

rorriM egamI—Mirror Image

I used to dislike mirrors until the night it cracked. They used to creep me out, imitating each action of mine, each movement so silently, as if it was a mime.

I remember that night when I put my hands down by my side and just looked right back at myself. That couldn't be me, though, I thought looking straight back at myself with hands tucked into the pockets, so deep as if hiding something.

I never liked mirrors, anyway. And this reflection only increased the dislike. Reflexively I punched at my reflection, causing cracks. I felt pain, not in my hands. There was no blood, there were no cuts and soon there was no man standing with his hands in his pockets. It was just me, trapped on the inside, slowly shattering and hurt.

I used to dislike mirrors, until I realized I wasn't the man, I was merely the mime artist.

Thirty Thousand Feet from Insanity

I'm sitting thirty thousand feet from the ground,
Subtle movement, no breeze, no sound,
Far from the real world,
Far from everything to which I'm bound.

Is this the feeling of achieving ultimate satisfaction?
No noise, no stress, no distraction.

Feels like I'm stuck in a bubble,
One free from all my tasks and troubles,
But something in me still feels incomplete,
I know this feeling is not permanent,
And there are still thoughts that are unwanted,
And I need to delete.

Even up here I can't escape any thoughts,
Along with my baggage even they were brought.
Closer to landing, the wheels get set to do their part,
It's time to turn off my autopilot.

No Quitting

You make an attempt, fate doesn't let you have your way,
Do you try again or just look away?

You try your best but only lose,
Should you try till you win?
Or just tie the noose?

You've tried it all,
Every method, every step covered,
Yet you fall.
Surely there is no hope,
Should you perhaps tighten the rope?

Maybe the time isn't right,
Maybe you aren't too bright,
Certainly that means it's time to give in,
Forget all the progress you might have made,
And all the dreams within.

But wouldn't that make you just another quitter?
Trying once, maybe twice,
Then giving up because life is too bitter?
I'm not going to follow the herd,
I might not be able to reach my aim,
But that doesn't mean my vision will always be blurred.

We

We're all sitting in this place,
Heading in the same direction but we're all in our own lanes,
Oblivious to what lies ahead.

We're all strangers in this place,
Only hoping to cut to the chase,
And get to where we're trying to be led.

But where are we heading to?
And how will we know?
When we reach where we've always wanted to go?

All part of one system,
All abiding by the same format,
We classify ourselves as humans,
Only to realize we're all robots,
Following this methodical way of life,
Mere puppets, definitely fools.

We started this chain of living,
These steps to achieve a life that's bliss.
We're all so focused on our final aim,
That we don't realize all the opportunities we miss.

We're all sitting in this plane,
All part of one game,

No clue who we all are,
But somehow we're still the same.

With no motive in mind,
Only a goal that pushes us from behind; we move ahead,
Like a boomerang,
We keep moving towards the light,
Only to return to where we began.

Waiting Lounge

$\mathcal{I}$ sit in the crowded lounge alongside economically sound beings with my broken foot held up high. It lies on a wooden table on which a wet glass of half-drunk beer is kept.

The painkillers made an absurd cocktail along with the wheat-based toxin that helped wash them into my swollen gut. Distended because of the heavy breathing from the constant flashbacks to the past. These once happy thoughts were supported by false forecasts of the future that is now as uncertain as life itself.

My body, now embraced from the inside by the warmth of my third pint, concocts imaginary scenes of how else my life could have panned out. I hated choices and today karma had done the inevitable; it had made me regret this uncalculated vengeance.

Cries start to increase in the waiting lounge that looks like a board room, as each resting traveller is disturbed by the most familiar sound to human ears. I look startled as I am brought back to reality by the tears that moisten her face as she spreads her petal soft arms in the air as a protest for not being entertained. Frozen by the ear-splitting noise, I find myself unable to calm her relentless plea.

Sitting in the corner of the half-lit, trolley-filled lounge, the two of us are now the centre of attention of the travellers whose eyebrows all rise together. I stretch out for my crutches to be able to eventually support and shield her from her despair that has never been this long since the four days since her birth. My tired arms are of no help, they shake more than a Parkinson's patient's arms, causing the crutch to slam into the mostly empty beer glass that spills froth onto the rug. This only reinforces that the other constant in my life has been failure, alongside death.

The noise sounds like a cymbal being hit. Ariana cries out loud enough to drown out the flight cancellation announcement. At this helpless moment I wish I too could scream at the top of my damaged lungs, without being judged. As I pull her pram closer to me, my plastered leg acts as an anchor supporting my half-stretched body. I sense a fear of this imbalance remaining like this forever. I cradle her in my arms, as the sniffling from her wet button nose lessens, indicating that her hunger for appreciation has been fed. Her tiny fingers, now stroke my arm with each snuffle, confirming for the fourth consecutive day that she too is a restless sleeper.

In all the disarray I forget the pain in my swollen, throbbing ankle that is stubborn enough to persist through the effects of pills and alcohol. I turn my left wrist gently to check the time. My arm is only weighed down by the ring on my finger which reflects a distorted figure back at me.

A swarm of people move rapidly, like bees, towards the departure gates in a disorderly manner. This waiting lounge houses thousands of individuals with thousands of stories, some identical to others. I wonder if anyone has one similar to mine. My phone reads 8.42 p.m.; the bright light burns my eyes which reminisce the past in frequent intervals. My reminisces are interrupted by a man with a wheatish complexion wearing a blue vest and a badge as lustrous as his slick, gelled side parting.

'It's time to board the flight. Sir, could you please give me your boarding pass.' His polite voice hypnotizes me to respond quickly, something I had not be able to do only a few moments ago.

'Will Ma'am join us on the flight directly or should we wait for her here, Mr Singh?'

I did not understand his comment. 'Of course my daughter will join us! Of course she will,' I respond, feeling angry. But my composure fortunately triumphs over my jet-lagged frustration at the man who had been assigned to push my wheelchair and daughter to the flight back home.

'Yes but she doesn't need a ticket,' I respond indicating my daughter who lies asleep as I wait to be pushed by the man who I had welcomed with a false smile, something I had mastered over the past four days.

'Not your beautiful baby sir. This lady whose picture fell out along with your boarding pass.'

I hold the picture of a woman, her hair streaked blonde, her eyes greener than spring touched grass and my mouth quivered, choking from the immediate dryness that occurs. As I cradle the girl who was the symbol of the sacrifices love forces us to make. I close my eyes to reassure myself the two of us have made the right choice.

'No, Mrs Singh won't be joining us; it's just the two of us from now on.'

Serenity in Chaos

These busy streets with headlights,
Looking over, act like ever present beacons,
Shining over these silent minds.

These silent minds with a heart beating near it,
Is a catalyst to the serenity,
Within to accompany the streets.

The Conditioned Air

The conditioned air serenades with its filtered breeze,
Aperiodic intervals open the doors,
To sounds of the rickety metallic cooling provider,
Violently vibrating as if gasping for its own filtered air,
While I stare at my own reflection,
Typing in an innate moment of chaos,
Accompanied by periodic bursts of despair.

The bulb shining over me flickers,
As if suggesting an epiphany,
The rain falling against the ceiling begins to tire down,
As if hinting at times of serenity ahead,
I look at the hours passing,
As I stare at the minuscule words,
My mind has managed to bleed.

These moments of silence instigate havoc within,
Questioning perpetually between what is to be or not to be,
Ultimately mixing up the difference between,
The good, the ugly, a blessing or a sin.

The mind corrupts itself,
Conning this intricate structure of lies to believe,
All that is around to be,
As pure as the conditioned air that numbs the face.

Separate but Together

We all think we're alone,
Until we open our eyes.

We all feel cold,
Until we embrace thy arms.

We all think today's problem is bigger than yesterday's,
We never appreciate each blessing,
Always wanting more.

We come together only when we are falling apart,
We make the most of the end,
Never embracing the start.

We fall, we rise,
We love, we despise,
Feelings keep the blood rushing in our veins,
Thoughts of love and hatred,
Making us more alive as they pass through our brains.

We think we're all together until we close our eyes,
We believe each word is the truth in times of need,
Even the crudest lies.

We open our eyes to know we're not alone,
We finally close our eyes,
To have only one name written on our gravestone.

So together we are,
Alone.

If Only

If life was as precious,
As every breath before going underwater,
If every moment we doubt ourselves,
It only becomes shorter,
If each moment isn't anything,
But a mere reflection of our dreams,
If only there was nothing such as singles,
And we were all just a team,
If we conducted each deed for ourselves,
And not just to succeed,
Only then we'd cherish each moment we breathe.

As I Lay Here

I lie here, half my body cold, like a teaser to the feeling that will soon take over me. I stretch, none of my movements outwardly visible, like an introvert desperately hoping to break out of his shell. I use the only muscles now functioning, straining my eyes to look around the blue room that seems to be mimicking the heavenly skies. It is covered with flowers and cards, as though to decorate a newly built coffin.

I overhear the nurse speak in a voice so mellow, it would be a whisper even if she used the loudest megaphone. She walks in to check the bottle of painkillers, the contents of which have numbed all the pain except the pain of my unfulfilled promises. My body is so heavily flooded with drugs that I feel like a guinea pig for these prodigies in white lab coats—a Frankenstein's monster in their lab, and a subject for their education.

Having lost track of the sun's movements, my day only begins once I hear the switches being turned on and off. Sometimes, I see the days and nights flash past my bloodshot eyes, when Sumer climbs up on the chair to cure his boredom with the help of the switchboard. I try and smile to express my joy but my body defies each of my movements, ultimately allowing two saline drops to run down my dry face from my dehydrated eyes, as I watch my grandson climb up the stool like it is a mountain in order to overcome my lifelessness.

The private room seems to smell like fresh air; the fragrance ironically provided by the tinned artificial air fresheners. There is an array of gourmet food—the hospital duplicating the services of a luxury hotel for visitors to assuage their grief. I, on the other hand, lie staring at a fan that rotates at several speeds in a motion waving me goodbye. I am constantly medicated through my moist oxygen mask. My morphine infused body fights hard to make sure I feel the itch and thirst from all the flashbacks that cause my exhausted mind to reel.

The television flashes bright white; it announces, *'Where there is life, there is hope.'* I stay horizontal, still, like a deer in the headlights, losing confidence in medical advancement.

She walks in through the door glancing at me with her hazel eyes, as radiant and gleaming as fresh honey. She approaches my four legged resting place. Using my peripheral vision, I see her hand stroke my arm pricked with needle marks. I keep my eyes closed envisioning what her soft, featherlight touch would have felt like against my skin if I was not as numb as my heart had been the second I fell for her. Her angelic image fades before my eyes, like smoke in the air; I sense the drugs wearing off. As these bitter chemicals leave my mind and heart, they release despairing hallucinations about moments I yearn for more than a gasp of fresh air.

A constant symphony rings in my ear, with a periodic, poetic rhythm to it. It reaffirms that I can still fight this lost battle. At times the melody turns into an aching sound when my body decides to choose my fate.

Despite my organs opting for an early grave, my senses seem to work overtime. I can see each and every one of my loved ones crowded around me during the days when I ache to speak and see their faces, instead of imagining them in my tired mind. On the days when they are caught up in their lives I remember how we would spend time, before I was trapped between these four walls. Playing cards, gambling, making bets we couldn't afford, my eyes squint as my muscles ease into a smile in appreciation of those blessed days.

I lay here, with these moments on rewind, flashing before my closed eyes. I am glad it was all planned this way because if I were to leave again, I'd hope to relive all the chaos that led to the harmony.

Window Pane

Sitting around, looking out of the window pane,
No sense being made, clearly a waste of time,
Still looking far into the night pretending it's all fine.

While I'm stuck in pause,
Someone else has pressed play,
Doing what I can, making it useless for me to stay.

Just because there are no bars around us,
Doesn't mean we aren't jailed,
Trapped in the past, weighed down like an anchor,
Even our thoughts have sailed.

Trying to find my purpose of being here,
A purpose to do something meaningful,
A reason to make my existence clear.
But while I sit in one place,
A million move past me at lightning pace,
Leaving me behind to find my way,
While I look out of this window pane.

Reminisces

Those long walks,
Those endless talks,
Those 1 a.m. drives,
The time I brought flowers to your place in disguise.

Talking about the future,
While we unwrapped the present,
Leaving trails of mud in the park,
Talking about all the journeys,
Which we wanted to embark.

Those drinks we shared,
Those nights,
Those nights were rare,
But they played a part indeed,
Like an animal out of its cage,
Completely free.

I wish I could reminisce about these moments till eternity,
This imagination is the remedy to the pain,
Caused by the times that could have been.

One for All, All for One

*D*opamine, a neuro-transmitter that is released from the brain, causing a chain reaction leading to the heart pounding three times faster than normal. The extra gush of blood finds its way to the cheeks and sexual organs. This sudden diversion of blood makes your stomach feel a bit empty, causing you to feel like you have butterflies in your stomach. All this for just one sentiment that unifies people and separates some. The most powerful emotion—love.

Love is a drug, one that is all around us but not easily available. It definitely isn't safe yet we're encouraged to spread it. In its truest definition, love can be compared to a rose. From a distance its loveliness draws you closer to it, luring and reeling you in with the legend of its beauty; but only when you hold it close enough do you feel the prick. It's the most powerful weapon to destroy someone, impacting the same parts of the body that are stimulated by cocaine. At least the effects of cocaine wear off.

I went too far and that was my mistake. I gave too much of myself to someone other than myself, and that's what made me trip before I had reached the finishing line. I tried too hard and this irony explains why love is the hardest question to answer.

However complex the brain might look, it can't solve the puzzle caused by the inner complications when we fall for someone. Thus it piles these thoughts into the same area where we could get addicted to them. It makes me wonder whether the brain is still the smarter one of the two or if the heart eclipses it.

I started off energetic and brave like an adrenaline junkie, constantly high on the rush that got me to say exactly what I believed and do exactly what she wanted—what we wanted. Eventually we overwork the mind and demand it to be responsible for another. Someone you deem more important than life itself. And then we point fingers and complain—love kills. I had overworked myself enough for my brain to play the kinds of games on me that would be illegal if it was playing them on another person. Our whole life is an illusion and we are the magicians deceiving ourselves that each of our actions is relevant in the long run and every emotion we feel is necessary; only one is, and we are most careful in sharing it and overly eager as we do. She was a victim of my need to share this emotion.

The rain played its part in bringing us together. I'd humour her each time, reassuring her about why we were meant to be together. The rain tapped on the roof of the sleek bus stop shelter, competing with my heartbeat as I inched closer to her. There was room for one more person and the anxiousness inside replaced this void.

'Strange whether, this rain,' my awkwardness was evident in my broken English.

'I love the rain,' her voice was melodious and interrupted by the pitter-patter of the rain.

'Yeah, me too. I love this rain. It's strangely…good.' In my desperate attempt to get her to smile I was like a schoolboy trying to cover up a lie.

At times the things that take us by surprise are the ones that don't surprise us when we respond to them so gracefully. She was the prime example of this.

She nodded as though appreciating our brief conversation. But I was stubborn enough to make another attempt as we waited for the bus. 'I think the campus shuttle might be stuck in the rain. It's usually always on time,' speaking with utmost confidence, I pretended to know the bus schedule better than a conductor would. I hoped for the conversation to stretch further than the previous one had. Her silent approval with a nod reaffirmed the coldness in the air.

'Are you going towards campus? We can share a cab if you don't mind because I'm heading towards Victoria Halls.' I stood persistently trying to return each silent reply until I had an affirmative answer, like a wall deflecting a ball.

'I stay right opposite, on West One; but no, thanks. I'm broke after this weekend,' her meek reply was inscrutable; her words indicating she was keen on sharing a taxi though her straight face contradicted the response.

'I'll cover it for now and you can give me your share some other time.' In control of the situation, I took the initiative to ensure a prospective second meeting.

Perseverance does pay off and this shared journey was my prize. After a short stint of persuading her to escape from this rain, hoping to spend additional time with her, we ended up under another common roof. Less than a kilometre away from the stop, we saw the bus drive past us, its headlights blinding us, making us pretend not to notice it. We sat less than a foot away from each other, cold and drenched. Our silence due to the inner tension provided the warmth. Smiling with mute signs of regard for each other, we remained quiet for most of the journey. It was as though we were playing charades. The taxi driver, who must have been a spectator to several interesting rides, was witnessing the start of a new story.

The wheels of the car glided along wet roads that splashed water onto the pavements. We dried off close to one another, but not close enough. After nine hundred seconds and ninety heartbeats per minute, we reached her student halls which was the image of perfect rained out Sheffield that had been marketed in the accommodation leaflets.

'Thanks for covering the fare, Rishi; here's my number. I'm Riana by the way.' Her name was music to my ears as she walked out, her hair, flowing down her shoulders, was like a waterfall. She smiled, looking at my bag which had my name scribbled on it. Our eight kilometre journey that was filled with words spoken from radio and the rain around us, ended in the name and number I had yearned for ever since we had been at the bus stop. For an avid table tennis player my reflexes were too slow, stopping me from making the moment last any longer.

Despite being a student on a tight budget, the six quid that she owed me was nothing in comparison to my anticipation to meet her again. I played my part tactically, waiting like an impatient child for two days before I could message her.

Being a university student had destroyed any concept of having a sleeping pattern or a schedule. I sat in the library among empty chairs and a couple more filled with nervous students on a Wednesday morning at 7 a.m. My eyes were deeply sunken in. Sleep deprived and anxious, I typed out my message to her four times over. Proofreading more times than I had for any assignment I pressed 'send' as my thumb quivered with the responsibility.

'Hi, this is Rishi. I've been in the library pulling an all-nighter for my marketing module and was going to head for a coffee before I sleep for a week. I'll put the bill on your tab at the cafeteria if you like or you could join me?'

I was hesitant about messaging her at such an unearthly hour for a 20-year-old. However, messaging now would give me enough time to get a reply and prepare my response. I pondered possible replies she could send to my sheepish attempt at being humorous. Worried she would think it was odd of me to have messaged her this early, or wondering whether it was outlandish of me to have messaged my plan as though typing in a journal, I felt burdened. 7.01 a.m. and I had not received a single text. One minute felt slower than an hour while I stared at my computer which was on sleep mode; I too should have been asleep. A television on mute would have made more sound than a library filled with books by authors, many of whom would have been the hopeless romantics I categorized myself as. My anxious thoughts were interrupted by a loud vibration that awoke the students who too had pretended to be immersed in revision.

'Wow, there is more than one person up at this hour! I'm on my way to campus for netball but let's meet in ten and I'll get you a coffee and some breakfast before you hibernate?'

Her message was like the exact opposite of a chill down my spine. I felt the warmth of relief from repeatedly reading the message. Her question was the easiest for me to answer and the lack of energy in my exhausted body was immediately substituted by a burst of adrenaline. My brain didn't need a caffeine rush to wake up and my body didn't need food to rejuvenate itself anymore.

Dressed in the university training kit, she wore shorts that ended just over her perfectly symmetrical knees with a cream sports jacket that matched her gravity defying ponytail. There was a hint of sincerity in her smile as we met in the café. It was just the two of us and two part time baristas who were the spectators to this morning encounter.

With the clock striking 7.30 a.m. and the sun having risen just over an hour ago, we were fresh and talked enough to compensate for the silence during our taxi journey. I savoured the overpriced, tasteless coffee and bagel that the café had stored overnight as 'fresh' products. In truth, I was savouring each word she said. We connected like two opposing magnets, agreeing and relating on any subject we brought up. From university timetables to our favourite tequila-influenced stories, we laughed together without keeping track of time. I handed her my favourite band which I wore on my wrist just so I had another excuse to meet her to get it back. As I made her wear it around her arm, I longed to hold on to and hoped she never took it off.

Over time, these dates to connect over coffee became a ritual. For two atheists, this was the only custom we had every Wednesday. I looked forward to them because of the coffee I had developed a soft spot for. The library soon became our meeting place. Amid words and literature, we created a story for ourselves, about ourselves. We met every Wednesday and my Tuesday overnight revision became a routine as I waited for the next morning's coffee. The caffeine did the job purely because of all the cups I had had staying up for the one I looked forward to. Even the baristas knew the time we would arrive, preparing the cups beforehand and eventually learning to take their time to serve us because they too realized that we weren't in any rush. These once-a-week sessions then turned into Sunday meals together in our respective flats and soon each day had a new meaning till we lost track of the days.

Our university days were spent together and every day we talked about a new subject. Although we had different aspirations, we chose to follow the same path in order to end up at a common destination. However, life doesn't pan out as smoothly as the road we first travelled on together. I got into a consultancy firm in London and she remained in Sheffield to work as an assistant vet. The two and a half hour distance between us couldn't get in between our relationship.

Over the course of our three years at university together, we got to know each other like sculptors know their sculptures. Fully aware of each line and curve in her body, I was a connoisseur and she was my 'specialised subject'. We spent every day together and soon twenty-four hours weren't enough. It's strange how it's hard to identify the very moment we fall in love and even harder to get out of it. We shared passions—from a favourite meal to our desire for listening to the Blues, a favourite cuisine; and most importantly, a shared passion for each other. Smitten by her every move, I was even more determined to succeed in life because it had taken on a new meaning. This was the sole reason why moving 270 kilometres south from her didn't faze me because I found a part of her in everything green, every Mexican meal, and every person I talked to. The dopamine in my body flowed like adrenaline every time I saw her.

Soon enough corporate life intervened, acting as a speed-breaker to the time we spent continuously together. Weekends became as anticipated as those Wednesday morning coffees. We alternated our visits and on the first and third week of each month it soon became the norm for us to be in the city that had brought us together. Each two and a half hour train journey spent to reach her was the rehearsal space to prepare all I could share within the next, much anticipated forty-eight hours. Soon the rest of the world became a blur and unimportant when it came to her. The distance away from her seemed painful. I felt choked by words that were waiting to be shared with her; but she wasn't around. Try going a week without speaking to a single person despite having enough to vent about. The exact feeling of frustration which tears into your gut and causes the acidic sensation when she arrives was the predominant state of my body when I couldn't speak to her. The red postbox outside my flat reminded me of her in a red dress, each morning. It was her honeyed voice that made me aware of the arrival of the underground trains. The wind was her way to whisper her affection and that got me through the day. Soon insanity seemed sane and addiction became a synonym for normal.

When we first kissed, each first kiss, I felt scared, nervous about whether her lips would reciprocate. That fear concocted with the chemicals that rushed took charge of my actions to make each moment recur.

I greeted each person with warmth as though they were Riana. I missed her less because someone had to be away for you to miss them; and she wasn't. She sat near me for post office drinks with the other colleagues and they loved her. Her flat was opposite mine and I wondered when we would move in together. She even knocked on my door, her bag packed, every second and fourth Friday of the month and I'd wonder where she had gone. Every day she smelt different and every day I smelt different too. I loved all her fragrances but I was most accustomed to her weekend scent because it made me feel nostalgic.

Soon, every day became as normal as the past three years had been. My year in London didn't seem as bleak with her by my side. Every day in the week had a new meaning again. I loved Mexican Mondays and Tequila Tuesdays which always led to Water Wednesdays, but I always wondered why she texted me from a new number each time. We were fond of alliteration and it was fond of us.

There was less to share over the weekends when I would want to lie back and put my feet up, but she didn't appreciate this. On weekends she seemed different. She seemed a lot like she had when we had both been in Sheffield and not like she was every day between Monday to Friday. Each relationship has a day off and off days soon became our second ritual. Like a game of jenga we were hanging on, shaking with the fear of the inevitable. We both could sense a collapse. No longer were the weekends our time to sleep in. We held on to each other but it was just me who really held on long enough to forget whose heartbeat had kept pushing me away. I could still hear her breath tickle my ears but no longer did it whisper my name.

'We're drifting apart, Rishi. I know it's obvious but it's not because we don't meet often. When we do meet, we aren't really together. Isn't the whole point of spending time together to make time for each other?' The chemicals in my body that had taken charge ever since I saw her must have started a fire in me; I felt a burning sensation in my gut from her despondent voice. Despite being able to see that this ship was sinking, I was not willing to jump off. How was that not enough to prove nothing had changed ever since this had begun? If anything, my feelings only increased to a point that even I was surprised to know I could feel so much for someone else. I found it absurd that she had ignored every day we had spent together. Every moment of the week was dedicated to her, even the messages during work hours. I had no words to justify my feelings towards her because the best way I could were through my actions.

'We do share moments and I give you all the time I can. From our weekly dinners and theatre on Thursdays. This, along with myself, is all I can give you,' I sounded like a salesperson selling a product at someone's doorstep. For once our relationship seemed like any other as I had to weigh why we should be together. With each word I spoke to her about her beauty, as though explaining to an artist about his painting, I wished she would find the deeper meaning behind all of them as they poured out in my voice, laced with misery.

'What dinners? Which plays?' her impassive reply took me by surprise. I felt hurt and dejected but I was stubborn and persevered in fighting for her yet again. Despite having to remember each daily activity we had shared together, she acted oblivious except for all we did on weekends. I felt psychotic. A drug addict constantly hallucinating. But the marks on my body, impressions of passion and love, didn't lie. They were the last resort, my proof about the unmeasurable bond we shared.

She had accused me of cheating! The woman I saw everywhere and in everyone, the person who knew more about me than I did, blamed me for jeopardizing our relationship. Her words were cold and eyes unmoving as she stood away from the bed we had laid on most of the week. I would have laughed crazily but she had never seemed more serious. Her words sharper than a butcher's knife, she raged furiously, ripping off the band I gave to her, over our first coffee. I tried my best to persuade her again, but this time it seemed a lost cause. We were at the perfect distance to kiss; all we had to do was to jump, in the way we had done before. But instead she shook her head and moved away, never to come so close again. The physical distance between us grew as her mind became clearer. She began to pick up all her belongings strewn across my room. I felt a sinking feeling in my stomach, speechless and oblivious about what had led us from being so comfortable in bed to her getting closer to storming out.

A stranger today can be your lifeline tomorrow. This erratic nature towards life keeps us on our feet just so we can be swept off by them. For years we yearn for an easy life, a simple one with no speed bumps. As soon as we move at a regular speed, we get bored. This boredom leads us to excitement. The same excitement then makes us crave simplicity. This constant demand is what makes us inhuman.

Her soft skin was now red with the tears I ached to see. She wiped them with her arms filled with her belongings that decorated my room as a constant reminder of her. Her hands were full of bags and her mind of thoughts; but she shrugged off my attempt at opening the door. She closed it quick enough for our entire relationship to play like a movie reel.

Everything once sweet can turn sour if it is not cherished. We need to relive each memory to keep the sourness from settling in. We need to be delusional because being sane all the time can lead to insanity.

Time passed slowly and each second that ticked away added a prick to the time we spent apart as the weekday began with the burning of my eyes tired from the sun. I found it hard to walk and I was unable to speak but I saw her again standing in her red dress outside my flat. I heard her voice announce the train arrivals. She was everywhere and in everyone. Monday nights were for Mexican and we went for our usual meal. Again her fragrance was different from when she had left my door over the weekend. We continued our ritual every day of the week, following the routine that my brain was used to, as familiar as writing. But the weekends shaped up differently. Like an addict without a needle, I felt incomplete.

I went to the train station to book my one way ticket to Sheffield and get answers to questions I hadn't dared to think about before. I sit here on this train, looking out of the rain splattered window, a hazy reflection of myself and the empty seat near me. I wish it was filled by her.

I find comfort in words as I type them, as if they were a vehicle bringing me nearer to her, though she seems further away from me than the moon, under which we both used to plan a future we had promised to one another. I type quicker each time I feel that prick inside me, constantly reminding me that my present will not be as beautiful as the past because the main ingredient is no longer in my arms. I comfort myself typing words which are filtered through my brain that has lost all hope; my heart has never felt so alone.

The heart is the most cunning organ. It makes the mind believe the thoughts generated in the brain; whereas the heart is the curator hoping for chaos because agony is its favourite drug. Only yesterday had I told myself that tomorrow would be a new chapter and yet I find myself remembering those four years, constantly forcing my thoughts back in time and stealing another glimpse of all our first times.

As I write what replicates another one-sided conversation, I hope to continue to write. I find comfort in these words that have no meaning, except for the enigma that each time I stop writing, I feel the distance between us increase. For me, you were always around and I couldn't hope for it to have always been just you. My mind played tricks orchestrated by my heart as I overdosed. Today I understand why love is a drug.

The dopamine in my body led me to hallucinate when the oxytocin in my body started to overflow making me see her in almost every woman. She thought she was just another girl, but she is the one for me. Recalling her green eyes and her, my two favourites, I wished to immerse my fingers in the valleys between her long and thin fingers that had an impression of my hand. Her eyes that always seemed to be filled with laughter peered out from over cheekbones that rose from a jawline sharp enough to cut the tension that had arisen before she had walked out of my door.

The right one. The one. The only. These phrases and reassurances from inside ourselves keep us afloat in a relationship. But as it drowns, we either find out it's the truth or a lie. But eventually, whether it works or not, we all always want the wrong woman. Not because of her qualities but the access. The lack of access and possibility drives us closer and intensifies the attractiveness in the moment that leads us to pursue her like a dog thirsty for water. I didn't want that. I just wanted Riana wherever I went. Fortune favours the brave and I was courageous enough to fall in love.

I didn't mean for this to have happened the way it turned out. Intricacies can complicate matters and that's what we learned about each other as we took steps down a forbidden road together. But we chose to forget this complication. Nothing simple is worth trying for. We mostly try so that we fail. Just to get back and enjoy the success even more as we hold it in our hands tighter than the skin binds the bones. A few seconds of happiness and ecstasy that lead to several moments of despair; and yet we go about injecting ourselves with these short-term highs in order to think about them when we are feeling low. All our needs and greed, every desire we itch to fulfill is a matter of time. Some can be achieved in time but some cannot.

All the little details collected within a private safe of the tiniest details that made her mine, like nobody else knew her, are the same details that devour me from the inside. Everything about her that I would love now makes me hate myself. I wish for them to play out in front of me once more. Every one of her habits that bothered me still does but only because they exist solely in my head.

I couldn't conceive that the rest of the women weren't her. She is truly unique but my stubborn and greedy heart ached to see her when it couldn't. I was deluded into thinking I was with her at all times and I would give back each weekday misspent with another woman for a weekend with her.

One-sided love stories are painful. Yet, they are what most people remember and what most never forget. I, too, am stuck, hurting inside, in need of screaming out so loud even she hears my pain—an expression of love that my eyes convey to her each time my gaze meets hers.

Is my story unique? Yes. All our pain and sadness is unique and that's what makes this beautiful mess so hard to resist and get rid of. Today I wish only this joy remained and not the agony that followed, which conjures memories that are now nightmares.

I feel tears close to streaming down my face that is ever so familiar with the dampness. I start to wonder whether all this pain is ever going to go.

Is it her fault for not helping me through this? Is it her responsibility to prevent me from feeling like this? I wish it was; at least then I could spend more time with her. Yet again I will count down the days till I hug her as if it were the last time. Now I wish I knew when the next time is.

Now I'm stuck with a room full of pictures of Riana. I'm terrified to pull them down because I hesitate, not sure which one is really her. With each metre this train moves forward, I continue writing and hoping the distance between us doesn't increase.

All this for just one sentiment that unifies people and separates some. The most powerful emotion—love.

Mirror

I stand here looking at you,
You look back at me,
Asking questions, making statements,
Promises of what could be.

Many come and go,
You share your secrets with me, with you,
I watch you smile, I watch you tear up,
But looking at you is all I can do.

I'll forever stand here,
Waiting for you to look at what you are transforming into,
I wait eagerly, remembering each face,
Each individual as they grew.

I'll ask for nothing in return,
Except for you to be true to me,
True to yourself,
I can only see what's outside,
Only you can see right through.

I often hope that the next time we speak,
Our one-sided conversation will fill us with joy,
I only hope,
You always see a clear reflection of yourself in me,
Because while I stand here looking at you,
I hope you fulfill all the promises you made me,
You made yourself.

Back to the Past

I remember when I used to pretend to be a cricketer.
Hitting a thousand runs a ball,
To everyone I was oblivious,
But in my head, I could never fall.

I can still hear the commentary,
When those two superheroes were in combat and fighting,
I could be in a room filled with burnt matchsticks,
But still switch on the light.

A couple of decades have played their part,
Guided me like guardian angels from the start,
But I seemed to have lost my way,
I stay away from times of glee,
Seek darkness in the brightest of days.

Where are those days,
When the only trouble was the one I caused?
Where are those voices,
That controlled this laughter,
While we played hide and seek,
Instead of finding constant flaws?

I used to run around free,
Each step leading to a wider smile,
Making my cheeks hurt,

I haven't felt that pain in a while.

I wish I had left bread crumbs while I travelled this journey,
In order to return to that locker filled with joy.

I remember pretending to score yet another century,
I still pretend,
But I rather it was like back then.

Time to Get Our Future Back

We lost a future architect, a future doctor, a future nurse,
We lost hundreds of bright minds,
Who, before walking their path, were made to disperse.

We lost a future sports person, a future prime minister,
A million lights went out,
With the loss of our brother and sister.

We lost a future writer,
We lost hundreds of god's gifts,
A million more lights went out,
The smallest coffins are the heaviest to lift.

We lost a future me, we lost a future you,
This pain will stay forever,
But the cause to it needs to be a taboo.

We need to rebuild that future,
For the architect who was taken away,
Find the antiseptic for the doctor,
Whose absence is the reason for this dismay,
We need to be the shoulders for that sister and brother,
A backbone for everyone, one united pack,
We lost our future,
And we need to get it back.

Viewing Gallery

*R*ain poured from the top of my shed, tapping continuously against the roof as if it were God finally allowing me to pay a visit. The skies as grey as the rim of the chimney where my child, for whom, my shoulders were the pinnacle of the world, used to eagerly wait for Santa to shower him with gifts. Headlights shone straight through the holes in my home; a constant taunt and reminder that I lived in a home made from worn-out, discarded clothes and cardboard. All this, accompanied by the constant symphony of the honking cars and the abuses that were exchanged between thousands of furious people; although I was the only one living crouched under a three foot tall shamiana, with a constant drip on my cemented floor, reaffirming that I was still breathing in this pollution and anguish infested body.

Ever since I claimed this corner of the pavement, I do not know when the sun's shift is taken over by the streetlights that stand tall over my head, as I strain my eyes sunken like the potholes near me, searching for him. The street lights acting as a searchlight with irregular flickers suggesting I give up.

No longer do I know what day it is, or what month. I don't see the need to because you don't book an appointment for where I want to go. I have learnt the date, time and location are decided for you. I wish I didn't have to learn.

I feel hail fall through one of the viewing galleries in my torn marquee, landing on the back of my head; adding to the chill down my spine from the thought of how my tiny mirror reflection would effortlessly throw snowballs from his tender hands. The chilly rain tickles me as it flows down my eyes, competing against the salty teardrops that stream down. They eventually join together as one, flooding me with memories which, although as sweet as nectar, sting me every time I taste them.

I look up to the skies, and scream in anguish—a feeling I am growing used to. I didn't care about any stares and insults I have attracted. This was my moment of grief, the numbness at his loss could never have prevented my eyes from turning as red as the shirt he had worn that day, leaving my face moist from all the tears that had his name on them. I wish I could drown in the small rivulets on the road created by the continuous showers from above. This downpour was most certainly him using his newfound heavenly toys, with peals of thunder replicating his imitation of a lion, the newest and last trick in his book.

At regular intervals I peep through these man-made windows in my shelter, in search of him hiding from me all this while, just so he could win. I hear a haunting screeching sound, a noise so familiar it results in my left arm stretching to the left; a reflex that wasn't as much help now as it had been then. I close my eyes in despair, as I feel his smile beaming on me as the sun dries out the rain.

Hunger/Greed

That ticking sound of every second that goes past,
Makes me sick of the idea of coming last,
Last in a race that I don't know I'm in,
In a competition where I'm competing
With the person within.

How I wish those seconds could reverse,
Instead they cause the two of us to only disperse.
How I wish I could go back to being younger,
Where it was just me and my hunger.
The hunger that made me strive for the best,
But while I leaped for gold,
I seemed to forget about the rest,
And I found myself cocooned in a shell,
With thoughts of victory,
And defeating the idea of defeat,
So deep in this puzzle,
I was cemented like concrete.

Stuck in these thoughts,
That constantly made me fast forward to what could be,
Causing me to miss the present,
Turning into a stranger to that person in the mirror I see.

Yet I feel my stomach rumble,
Yet again I feel this hunger turn into greed,

Making me chase after the idea of victory,
Making me feel the absence of something I don't need.

Now with every second that goes by,
I hear that person in me die,
And I often get confused,
About which one I am today.

Someone Once Told Me

Someone once told me, this life isn't easy,
I looked at him and said,
'Brother, why are you hiding in this shed,
When you have your life to live ahead.'

With a quivering voice he cried,
'Look around, you will see,
Grief and sorrow,
With an abundance of poverty,
Bullets and curses shot at one another,
We're all actors, faking smiles,
And stabbing our own brothers.

We live our whole life paying bills,
Chasing fame and money are the values we instill.
What are you going to achieve by being out there?
There's enough room in this shed.
To hide from this inescapable nightmare.

Are you going to join the government,
Who claim to 'protect' us?
Instead, fight against each other,
And let our world rust.

At least this shed gives me a roof over my head,
Protects me from the storm approaching,

Delays death.

The world out there is nothing but a sadistic joke,
People give speeches to hide their sins.

But I figure you think you're the chosen one,
To change this demonic hell on earth,
I may warn you that many have tried to walk this path,
And yet,
The evidence of the impact they had lies in front of you,
But I'll wish you all the luck for what it's worth.

The Secret

$\mathscr{A}$ secret is a conversation usually among two people that remains between them; the message is not conveyed to anyone else. The reason I am in this unearthly state is due to a secret that was shared not only between two people but amongst the two thousand that live in my village.

Whoever this may concern,

I want you to know that I didn't come from a wealthy family; instead our source of income was from the pension that my family and I lived on. We received it because of my deceased brother, whom I hope to reunite with soon. I am not a bad person, at least not according to my definition of bad. All I wanted was to provide my elderly parents and my two younger siblings with some bread to eat and a roof over their heads to call their home; and if my actions still make me seem evil, so be it. I know what I did cannot be called moral or legal, but if no one had found out about it, then would it still be wrong?

I haven't completed my schooling school; not many in my village had. I had to leave school after we were informed of my brother's death in the war. It was the circumstances that made me bail on education, not my lack of interest or understanding. Since then, I looked after the household by earning money either through odd jobs like polishing people's shoes or, in more desperate times, begging on the streets. One summer morning, luck finally came my way when a man whose shoes I was polishing asked me to join work in his textile factory. According to him I was *'wasting my time'* polishing shoes and having me as an employee would be worth it, based on how hard I had worked at making his shoes gleam. I didn't hesitate for even a split second before grabbing this grand offer. I had finally reached my brother's status and had earned respect in my village; I became the sole breadwinner in my family, earning enough to educate my younger brothers and providing shelter for my parents at the same time.

Everything seemed too good to be true, and it was indeed. Industrialization made its way through India and workers were starting to become redundant due to the emergence of machinery. As luck would have it, I was one of those workers.

Just like the others who lost their jobs, I did not have family wealth to fall back on; I had been the backbone of my family. Thus I reacted fiercely; some would say I over-reacted. I rushed into my boss' office and asked him why he had picked on me when I had given my heart and soul, working overtime and had taken on more shifts than any worker in the factory. He answered quickly, contradicting every word he had said when he had appointed me. He explained in his gravelly voice, 'Son, you are wasting your time working here; you don't have it in you.' I couldn't control my emotions and using the same pair of scissors with which I cut cloth, I slit his throat and immediately fled from his office.

Bizarrely enough, the investigations couldn't find any sign of murder. His death was considered suicide and no one was blamed. I, on the other hand, ran away from home and alcohol became my only support. I had lost my conscience. I wanted to live for myself and all this insanity made me forget about my family, who were helpless without my assistance. I didn't have anyone to talk to until I made my very first friend, Tanya. She is the only person I will name because if it wasn't for her I wouldn't have learned to love and care for others again and tried to get back on my own feet. Coincidentally, we met outside the same textile factory I had worked in before. I grew to like her, not only because I was lonely but because she could see beyond my wretched state and was curious to know me. I saw her coming into my life as a second chance. I didn't need alcohol to fall back on in times of misery. Not only was she my only friend but the woman I would have married if I hadn't been such a wreck.

I started to ignore my past and worked as a stationmaster to earn enough money and respect to be worthy of marrying Tanya. I moved in with her and with every day together, the trust between us grew stronger and so did the guilt of murdering the man who had fired me from my first job. My conscience became a companion to the sensation of love; an emotion I thought had been destroyed far beyond repair. I had to tell someone. I couldn't keep it to myself anymore; the shame and remorse of murder was killing me. The only person I had in my life was Tanya and I was concerned that she'd leave me after finding out the truth. But she was the only person I could tell and she deserved to know what had led me to become the person she had first met. Only a few nights ago, after I returned from work, I told her about the felony I had committed. She wasn't as concerned as I thought she would be but she made me repeat my story to her three times over, with each and every detail. I begged her to keep this a secret between the two of us and I couldn't have been more relieved when she said she would. The very next morning, I couldn't find my Tanya anywhere. I was worried. I thought she had left me for being a murderer but it was worse. She turned out to be the only daughter of my victim and the story spread around my village like wildfire.

You do not know me, but I hope you understand what led me to kill myself. This note is not because I left my deprived family alone, it's not because I killed a man and it's not because I am wanted by the police. I am doing this because what had been a secret between two people became a secret between two thousand.

Bus Stop

I was left waiting by the bus stop,
Standing alone in the crowd,
Slowly snapping back to reality,
Close to screaming out loud.

You, you were sitting in the bus,
He was sitting where I should have been,
We were moving further away as the distance increased,
If only you could have seen.

He said words just to make you smile,
It was only a matter of time till he got what I wanted,
The distance continued to grow with each mile.

Where had I gone wrong then?
Was it my speed?
Was I too naïve?
If you're too far from reach,
Why am I still finding it impossible to be freed?

He starts to play with your hair,
As an excuse to remove a thread,
He gently slips closer to your side of the chair,
You realize his intentions,
Move back an inch or two,
Finally, you were thinking about me and you!

He doesn't get the hint,
He continues to play with your hair,
Not realizing your objection to his previous attempt,
But this time, you smile,
Tilt your head to the side,
I realize that for you I would leave everything aside.

A feeling of heat develops in my chest,
A piercing pain a bit to the left.

I start to realize I had taken it too slow,
I shouldn't have fallen for your eyes,
Your ignorance towards me,
At the start of this one way admiration,
I should have been more like him,
Who is almost as close to you now,
As you are to yourself,
Instead of continuously being satisfied,
By misleading hallucinations.

I look at this sight in agony,
Because while I watched where I should have been,
For you,
I was left waiting at the bus stop.

Move On

Move on.
Move to the left,
Move to the right,
Time to take off,
And take flight.
That time has come and the minutes that have passed,
Haven't been added to the clock,
It's that moment to lift the anchor,
And finally leave the dock.

Eighty-one Cups to Go

$\mathcal{I}$ sipped on the coffee, this time a bit slower than before, desperately hoping for the straw to slow each sip, periodically scheduling each time my palate appreciated the caramel. I pretended to walk down, back and forth, each time slower, appreciating the scarce selection. In reality I was admiring what the reflection showed. I felt a bit daft, pretending to type numbers, attempting to magically guess those that I truly wanted. But with each sip I reduced the coffee and the chances of brewing something. With every gust of wind caused, when the door opened either way, I try to fool others that I am waiting for someone to fill the chair situated opposite me, exactly adjacent to whom I hoped would fill that void. Continuously pretending to stretch my neck to get another look, but with each moment the ice in my cup melts, I still haven't been able to break this ice. I find myself duping only myself by creating stories in my head, a story with just one character. Just like my straw, painfully attempting to get each sip of the coffee from the bottom of the cup, I discover myself trying to extract each moment from this untitled one-sided affair. 'People are created to fill a hole left by someone else,' I overhear a barista very wisely say to another while pouring coffee beans out of a bag, filling in the empty spaces in the machine. Was I the only one in the café to hear this? Why did I only hear that one sentence and nothing else? In the midst of this internal conversation with myself, I didn't realize that the reason I had been typing this somewhat monotonous piece, had left. But then I guess, what the barista had said had been accurate because with the same swing of the door, that spot near the empty chair opposite me was occupied by another reason to refill my cup.

The café would shut in another seven hours. The world record for the most cups of coffee consumed in that time is approximately eighty-two. I had eighty-one more cups to go and I was only hoping I wouldn't be sitting there long enough to break that record.

Lost

I'm just a lost man sitting in the dark,
Waiting for this torch to light up with a sudden spark.

I'm just a wanderer walking all alone,
Waiting by the side road,
Hearing my own moan,
And I know that you will be,
Lost without me,
But I wait for this light,
To take me home.

And I know where you have gone.
It's far, far too long,
But I know we will find this light.

So hold on tight and hold me close,
Close your eyes and give me that pose.

And shout out now,
So I see,
Where you have been hiding from me.

Where do I begin?
Where do I start?
When do you know if it's time to depart?
Where are the questions and where are the answers?

If this world is a stage,
Where is the performance with all those dancers?
Waiting for me to arrive,
On those holy nights,
And where do I begin,
To end this quest?

Why do I not know,
What I want to know?
And when do I find,
All that's lost?

Now I see you,
And I haven't a clue,
Why you're still waiting at that door,
That had been closed from much before.

Born in Debt

We're born with a debt,
Born with a loan to repay,
A reason not to go astray.

We're born for a reason, some say,
Others believe we're born to meet someone special one day,
Someone who will make everything seem set,
A stranger at first,
But later someone you will never be able to forget.

What if I lose the key to this lock,
With all the answers behind?
What if my aim is clear but the journey is hard to find?
What if every time I close my eyes,
That person is on my mind?

We always look for what we don't possess,
Making our life into a balance sheet,
Always thinking our pros and cons must be assessed.

This life is given to us on loan,
What we do with it is how we repay our debt,
What we remember will be our main asset,
We're sent astray in order to find our way,
Because every time we fall,
It's so we can learn how to stand tall.

Dead Man Talking

Why is he just lying there? It's getting colder, yet I can feel something warm dripping from my head. Maybe it's this situation that's making my head feel this way; I don't exactly know how to react.

What am I supposed to do right now? Am I supposed to climb down on the tracks and pick him up and move him like he's just a thing? I guess he is just a thing now; yet I can't get myself to move, stuck here as a spectator with a score of people finally realizing what really caused the delay. I guess we can't blame the lack of efficiency for the Underground's delay. We all might just be fortunate enough to reach work late or, even better, not have to go to work with this incident as an excuse.

I feel pathetic thinking this way; those who could hear me would probably prefer to put me in the place of what looks like a man in his mid-twenties with a brand new striped shirt, now red with a thick coat of his own blood and documents scattered all over his body.

I can't get myself to say a word, shell-shocked by the incident. I feel overly intrigued, wanting to know what had caused this freak accident. Maybe it's because we are all stuck in this packed station due to what seems to be someone's deliberate leap to the wrong side. But then maybe the cleaners hadn't cleaned up so well and he had slipped. No wonder there isn't any station staff in sight. Or he was pushed by someone who hadn't been aware of what he had done. They do say the London Underground is one of the busiest places during the morning rush hour.

Seven minutes have passed now and neither one of us has moved. The rest of the crowd seemed to have found something to do, while I am at the end of my story much before I would have wanted it to end.

Disbelief starts to escalate in my lifeless body, as it gets colder with each swipe of the cloth that the paramedics use to wipe the blood from his mutilated body, as if erasing the strokes of a masterpiece. It feels like I'm holding my breath under water; my lungs bloating with air, as I try not to exhale. I feel an icy breath tickle the back of my neck. I hear faint voices whispering around me. As they prepare to lift him up, a gust of wind seems to escape from his body, resonating like a sigh of relief, an escape from the life that made him anxious enough to wait for the train on the track itself.

Now elevated in the air, my hands dangle, drifting away from the days that led to this inevitable act. My body feels much lighter than it did ten minutes ago, the thoughts now fading away like the smoke from my last cigarette. I watch myself, wishing I had worn a different shirt to stain.

Desolate

A constant sound echoes in my ears,
With each mountain crossed I reminisce about those years,
Smiling to myself about where I sit,
With the other side blue, hoping for it all to fit.

I was never good at puzzles,
And today I wish that wasn't true,
Feeling desolate desperately searching for a clue.

Anxiously waiting to be shown the light,
How I wish I had valued every moment of respite.
Understanding my weakness,
Reinforced the thing which meant the most,
If there was a way to volunteer on my own,
I'd happily take the post.

Fear is a four letter word,
But not the four words I want to live with,
Love, however, comes along,
It's ironic how we become weaker,
As love becomes strong.

When

When will that door knock right back at me,
Because of which my knuckles are bruised,
The one that got me down on my knees?

When will that girl walk and say those words out loud,
The line I rehearse every day,
But can't spit out?

When will we get the questions,
For the answers that we find,
Looking for that eternal light,
Even though it's made us blind?

When will I be the person I aspire to become?
While I curse myself every day for something I haven't done?

When will I know that search is now done,
That this level named Life is finally over,
And I have won.

I sit here on this ledge,
Waiting for that door to knock.

From Start to Finish

*'You can't make anyone happy; you can just show them the
path that leads to it.'*

He had always counselled me with this famous line which
was synonymous with his personality. Constantly helping others
before he tended to himself. A good example of a sponge
when it came to soaking in others' sorrow. He absorbed all
their negativity and sprayed them with drops of happiness and
wisdom that would give them what he called 'five minutes of
eternal happiness', It was a mantra he lived by. 'A happy life
is one in which even a few seconds of true laughter outweigh
the years of tears.'

I'll never forget the day he first introduced himself to me.
It was the first day of school and a swarm of crying 4-year-
olds stood glued to their parents, afraid of the unknown future
that was before them. With his hair ruffled perfectly over his
small forehead he startled me, shoving me in the back with his
bright blue Power Rangers water bottle. 'That's a nice house
but not as nice as this one'. With one swift movement he
dismantled my foot-long Lego structure and placed the Lego
bricks horizontally across the red marbled floor. His explanation
before he introduced himself was that, 'This way everyone in
class can stay together.'

He is the same even today, despite the changes; all his
childhood softness has been replaced by sharp edges and
chiselled lines. The same dimple appears each time he laughs;

a laugh which is evident in his eyes which change to a vision of relaxed joy each time his head moves back, soaking in his glee.

At first we weren't the best of friends, purely because I was too shy around his upbeat personality, but he always looked out for me. From the time I forgot my packed lunch in the bus, when he shared every crisp in his box with me, to the day he was punished with me even though he had finished his homework, just so I 'wouldn't have all the fun alone outside'.

When we were in the fifth grade, we both fell for the same girl. She had curly locks that fell across her face when she got her first spot; her hair was a curtain to hide the imperfection on her otherwise radiant, rosy face. 'How about we race and the winner gets to sit in class with Sana?' he proclaimed in his signature enthusiastic tone during lunch break, as he knelt like he was a professional sprinter. He knew I was quicker than him and only once the race had begun did I understand why he had cast himself as bait for me. 'Ready, get set, GO!' He leapt one step forward as I ran metres past him to reach the school canteen, only to find myself running all alone. When I panted back to class, confused, I saw him speaking to her with a sideways grin that only I could see. That very day, Sana asked me out to the end of summer prom. I still don't know what he had told her but I'm glad the two of them hadn't gone off together.

All these thoughts from the past whirl in my head like an album compiled from my favourite pictures. Every time I think of these distant memories, he is an important influence for my fondness for them. With all the lessons I have been taught over the years I have known him, he has been a man of his word. He practices everything he preaches and he has helped push away my sorrows. Only last night over dinner did he say, 'Let's achieve everything that we have planned as quickly as possible. Time waits for nobody.' This impatient and enthusiastic approach to every coming second excites me about what is in store. I can't wait to make this the best journey possible.

Just like the beginning of our friendship hadn't started with a conventional handshake, I wanted to raise an extravagant toast like he would. I was eager to let you all know Dave the way I do. So since we are each other's best men today, I'd like to raise a toast to my friend, my mirror and my soon to be husband, Dave.

I do.

Hope and Prepare for Anything

Standing watching the water flow,
As it cascaded down the mountain side,
He leaned forward in pain to touch it as it streamed away,
Reminiscing every moment,
While creating illusions about each day.

With each passing day, the sun dried out the bay,
He was now a new man,
Still the same,
Still creating illusions,
But this time he didn't have a plan.

Above and Away

Here I sit thousands of feet away from the ground,
No honking cars, not much sound,
But one thought follows me up to the clouds,
Up in the tranquillity.

I wait here for the destination to arrive,
Over a hundred people around,
Our destinations are different,
Despite where we are bound for.

Are we strangers then?
Or are we clones of one another?
Are we competitors?
Or are we mirror reflections of each other?

Thirty-six thousand feet above,
And that one thought flies along,
Amongst the clouds now,
But these thoughts pull me back down.

We start to descend,
Closer to where we ought to be.
Wheels extending,
Destination in sight,
Maybe we all need to lose our sight in order to see.

No Light at the End of the Tunnel

Thinking back now, I remember I was sitting in my room. It was only a few more weeks until university ended. I looked to the left, I saw the mirror. I looked to the right and I saw a picture of myself. Then I gazed out of the window. Yet again, in the distance I saw my own reflection looking out for answers that weren't really there. A list of questions stacked up like jenga blocks, waiting to fall. I didn't really know where I was, not physically, but where I stood in this race with seven billion others. Others were heading towards the podium whereas I was lost finding my way to the starting line.

I remember I tried shouting out loud but nothing came out, nothing! Like running on a treadmill, it only felt as though I was moving forward. This just aggravated the confusion that was building in me, slowly causing me to question my sanity. I was at that stage where I wasn't sure on which side of the mirror was the real me; I still don't know which one questions the answers.

Frustrated by every reflection, I would wake up each morning only to wait for the sun to set. This day was different. This was not just any Friday and I certainly wasn't out there letting the alcohol take over my blood; not even that illusion could be of any help. I was getting sick to my stomach but there was no cure! It is a bit hard to find one when you turn out to be both the patient and the doctor. At times I wondered if this was all an act that I was putting on to get sympathy from everyone. It wasn't. I still didn't know what it was, what it is.

I looked around my room for inspiration but it didn't help. All those pictures just reflected images of a person I can barely remember, as if it was a delusion. Looking around that space was like wanting to free yourself from jail.

I still remember that night. It doesn't feel too long ago because not much time has passed since then. Of course there have been a few inevitable incidents. I am not going to go into any details; I'll let you decide my story, which unsurprisingly I shared with no one else but the man on the other side of the mirror. You have enough time to spend on your own and this mind is an interesting companion. It can make or break you, I'm sure you know which path it chose for me.

If you've found this piece of paper, please put it back behind the hole by the bed. Death row is a morbid journey.

What's Next?

Ever since I wrote my last promises,
Those ones the summer time,
People always ask me,
'Sanil, when is your next rhyme?'

Ever since those last drops of ink were used,
The ink for the rhymes indeed,
It seems like my imagination has ditched me,
A bird finally freed.

What can one choose from?
When their box is as good as new?

No past memory,
Giving others the opportunity to brew.

So, I ask myself,
Sounding a bit crazy I admit,
'What is your next work?
Or were those promises the last of it?'
Are you going to write a story?
Or is poetry your forte?
Maybe you can write about your future ambitions,
Or the times you went astray?

'How about you find some rhymes,

For all those global issues you want to eradicate,
Or about your childhood crushes,
That always got you to fixate?'

Some ask whether I said too much at once,
Whether I got greedy using everything I had,
Ultimately looking like a dunce.

Those voices make irregular appearances,
Just to pull me away from feeling strong,
But whenever they visit,
I write them a new rhyme,
Just so they don't tag along.

So, what follows after these promises?
Is it just a few more?
Maybe a poem about any hindrances faced,
Which I can't even recall anymore.

The question that rarely occurs,
And a question that makes me think,
'Is there another piece of work in me?
Or did the previous fill me to the brim?'

It gives me shivers to contemplate,
At twenty-three I might be speechless,
Was making all those promises a wise decision,
Or just another blunder, I need to reassess?

What if that were the last of my ammunition?
What if I was so engrossed in those words,

That I fell off the edge while chasing my ambition?

So, what is next in line?
A trendy song?
An enticing novel?
Or another set of poetic promises?
Maybe I need some time out to refill my pen,
Travel the world,
Fulfill my goals,
Before I write about another phenomenon.

A few more promises might be in store,
Lots of paths will be travelled to open the right door,
But what remains constant is that,
The show will go on,
Because we need to keep striving to reach the best,
In order to prove why we're born.

Silent Glares

Silent glares, a couple of more cheeky stares,
A sense of awkwardness, despite no collision,
This journey sure is helping our peripheral vision.

A conjunction of two songs serenade the two of us,
Turning this into a blind date,
The tension between us could cut through a diamond,
If it was up to me and you.

A door opens in front of us,
We both keep our heads embedded in our phones,
Wait for the next destination,
Exchange uneasy smiles after great hesitation,

Should I have greeted you good morning?
Will it be weird if I say good riddance?
Your presence starts to fade,
Despite the short distance.

We have lived many stories together,
Despite there being none between us,
This journey is making me realize,
Why this man-made box we're in makes everyone hush.

Alas, the door opens for me and you,
I step back, you step on my foot,

This klutzy situation continues as we complete our descent,
We share our last moments with sighs of relief,
As this elevator journey finally ends.

Dinner with the Turners

A feeling of claustrophobia kicked in every time I had to push and shove my way into this room. It seemed overcrowded the moment I set foot in the four-walled excuse for a home.

'You're going to London! Oh my God! You're going to have a crazy time, yaar!'

'London! I am so jealous, bro!'

'You'll be living in the palace like a king!'

As a teenager, midway through eighteen, these were the false assumptions I had been excited by the moment I subtly announced I was going to the London School of Economics for my undergrad. Subtle because my sly attempt at fishing for attention and likes only roped in twelve thumbs up. For a class topper with 97 per cent that was an average score but twelve more than before.

My group of friends envied me for securing a scholarship. After spending three years in this wet city, which for many is a country in itself, completely ignoring any other surrounding counties, I am soaked, like a sponge filled with hatred. Unlike my neighbours who snapped me up for their daughter's marriage the instant they heard I would be getting a UK visa, I was certain I wouldn't be putting up at the Buckingham Palace. I was eighteen and they had already stamped their visa approval on their daughters' chastity belt. It's safe to say the word 'Britain' still plays a large role in securing superiority over certain Indians.

Over a thousand days in the land of royalty and I have been living like a peasant with the aspiration of working my way up the ranks in a steep hierarchy that is taller than my girlfriend's family, at an average of five foot eleven inches.

Coming from a country where the average height is five foot five inches, I am an average man in all aspects and my height can vouch for this. An 'aam aadmi' for popular interest. However, dating a 20-year-old who hails from a country where the average height of a woman is five foot ten inches, whom you'd turn your head 360 degrees to see, I have punched not only above my weight but height as well. Often I am asked if I am insecure about these visible distinctions and I am not. Why would you question winning the lottery if you haven't bought a ticket?

I loved being away from home. The freedom to do anything you want with no restrictions and time constraints made me feel free to accepting this country as my own. The exchange rate and visa issues, on the contrary, were a clear enough signal that I was restricted economically and legally.

In a room where I had to shove my way around two small desks and a camp bed (the latter serving the purpose of a third desk when I wasn't in it) is what I called my student accommodation on most days. At 21 years old and four months before my finals, the real test was approaching; my visa was nearing its expiry as was my right to freedom. Surrounded by walls that hugged me close enough that my accommodation could be called an overpriced coffin, I walked back and forth from nervousness and lack of space; our pictures and her collage of selfies stared at me from the wall. The only comfort that kept me sane was Khan Saab and his good fruit and vegetable prices. They were priced even better if the customer was Asian. Situated right under my room on the busy streets of an East London borough, he sat behind his counter always trying to lure in customers by screaming product names. Despite having been in the country for over twenty years, he hadn't gathered that being less intrusive was a better sales strategy than the constant screaming about deals that woke me up every morning as they echoed up to my cramped, first floor cell.

I had been dating Dian for close to three years and I had been invited to her family Christmas dinner for the first time yesterday. The festive and chilly winter season sent cold sweats down my spine as I rehearsed my lines like an under-qualified candidate being interviewed for a job with too many requirements. I loved being around her family. I looked up to them, in all aspects, really. Luckily and thanks to my genetics, I wasn't the shortest, not by a long shot. Timothy, was shorter; of course he'd grow. It was only a matter of a year or two and he'd be my height but till then I was just about towering over a four-year-old. I couldn't be too proud of that, purely because they loved him more than Romeo had loved Juliet, I assumed. It was a different sort of affection, of course; but to quantify, it made the legendary lover look like a roadside Romeo for a change.

This was the first time I was going to meet the whole family together. I wasn't a nervous person by nature but when you have been convinced your own name is 'Koonal' and not Kunal, you tend to become apprehensive about meeting people who have the ability to make you doubt your own identity.

'Hi, I'm Kunal. Your daughter's a very charitable woman.'

'No, I'm not sitting down; this is me on my toes.'

'I'm Koonal. The proof that your daughter has bad taste.'

My clogged mind came up with all the possible outcomes that could not happen during my first official encounter with the Turners. My anxiousness and heavy head was given with a gentle pat as frequent showers of plaster fell on my neatly combed hair from above my low ceiling. The falling of the white dust was synchronized with faint moanings. Absurdly, this frequent occurrence over the past three weeks was not the top reason to despise this one bedroom flat that I had lived in for the past month. The top concern causing the severe frustration and restriction was Dian's disapproval at my inability of moving into a place that had 'panache'. Since the first time she had visited and had stated she would rather stay in an Indian prison than visit again, I had been denied the basic right in a relationship. Sexual frustration will always top the charts for a 21-year-old man with finals approaching and job interviews lined up.

I had preferred my previous room. It had been much bigger and I could stretch my short arms enough without touching either side. But with a conversion rate of 102 rupees to a pound, my pockets had never felt lighter. In order to make the most of the scarce space I took small steps as I paced around the room wearing a red jumper that was tucked into my new pink trousers; my clothes would scream westernization if I had chosen to wear it in Delhi. There were two hours till dinner and my anxiousness had led me to get ready too eagerly and early. I listened to motivational music as a means to build up my confidence.

'*Believe in yourself, as life is hopeless without hope...*' the husky, muffled voice, which spoke like a dictator narrating utter rubbish, was overpowered by the sound of the bass. A guitar solo muffled the tasteless inspirational lines. The low-cost recording that seemed to have been recorded with a towel over a microphone was interrupted by a loud knock on my door that was punctuated by a dry cough. Whoever it was, knocked three more times before I could open the door.

This box-sized room at £150 per week was the reason I did

not feel homesick. Just like back home, the ceilings cave in ever so often with a constant shower of plaster, whitening my hair before time, and I can hear Asian men screaming out product prices outside my window.

As I opened the door, I was greeted by a man wearing what seemed to be every colour we are taught during primary school. With more rings than fingers and sunglasses that reflected my image, he balanced the glasses on his forehead as it held each hair that was gelled back. He leaned against the door with a green bag in his left hand and a leather satchel hanging off his right shoulder.

'You need to open up quicker, my friend. I don't got all day for you,' he spoke in a sour manner as he analysed my appearance scornfully.

'Here's your stuff. Now the money, quickly! I have places to be for all those who need me,' he sniggered as he finished his awful attempt at rhyming. With each word he said, his personality shone through.

'Are you new at the shop? Khan Saab never mentioned you,' finally I was given a chance to speak as he gasped for breath after his strange monologue. I was concerned looking at the man who could have potentially taken the part-time job that would have provided me with enough pennies to move into a slightly bigger hellhole.

'Are you already high, mate? And what are you dressed like bud, pink with red? Are you dressing up as a fucking chewing gum or what?' his response was sardonic, completely ignoring my question. He was now playing stylist to my lack of fashion sense. His informal tone and instant comfort with me stirred a sense of uneasiness.

'He never mentioned he was hiring. You got hired and I

didn't?!' I didn't believe it. I handed him heaps of change in return for the bag of groceries covered in newspapers.

'Do you get paid for this?' shyly I asked, with jealousy underlining my question.

'Of course I get paid, who else do you think grows your greens at the farm, eh? Anyway, let's smoke some bud soon,' he walked off putting his shades on like a disguise to his cunning offer, leaving me muddled in confusion.

'I don't do drugs,' I lied, shouting across the hall as if I was under surveillance by the visa officers who would take note of this lie I tried to cover up.

'Yeah and I'm not a drug dealer,' he vanished in the darkness of the dimly-lit hallway.

Left confused and offended by his insult about my dressing sense, I felt naked from the insults. I was shirtless, looking for a plain white shirt that wouldn't attract any undue attention. Being a student makes you value money more than life itself. Although we wouldn't have a life if it weren't for money, I still rated the worth of the latter as much superior. I respected money in a somewhat spiteful manner due to limited access to it. I became more careful in my purchases, from making cornflakes my dinner on weekdays and breakfast on weekends (because we all deserve some pampering). I stretched over my bed-cum-table to pick my multipurpose blazer off the washing-line-cum-open-closet as my phone began to vibrate and move more vigorously than the reason causing the white substance to shower from above.

'Hi babe! Wait, what? Why are you yelling? I can't understand. No, I didn't forget to call before leaving. I haven't left. Wait, what, why're you getting hysterical, we're meeting in two hours and I'll be there twenty minutes before that. It only takes twenty-five minutes from Piccadilly Line,' I replied frantically hoping I wasn't going to be sentenced to the hell I would be given on the other side of the phone.

'What do you mean we meet in forty?' I checked my watch. The realization I would not be able to get out of this mess started sinking in as I start talking much quicker over her peeved voice.

'My watch is stuck! This damn watch is absolute shit! No, you're not, babe! The watch! The watch, not you! Why would you be shit! Yes, yes, you got the watch but you didn't make it, na? Anyway, I'm leaving now. I just need to change. Wait I can't wear that jumper, it's too small now. I know it's festive but I'm sure your mum will understand if I don't wear it. Fine, I'll wear it.' Holding a Christmas jumper that would hug my body like skin and suffocate me like the walls in my room, I started to put on the reindeer infested woollen menace. It made me look like I was desperately trying to fit into English society.

'Wait, and the scarf? But it's pink! Apparently red and pink don't match,' caught between two contradicting fashion tips, I was forced into wearing the pink scarf that highlighted my attention-seeking outfit.

Bollywood films teach us that love is all about sacrifices but they never show the protagonist giving up his personality and dignity!

I had never been good under pressure and started to panic and hurry up before leaving. Back home if I had invited Dian to a family dinner, my entire extended family would have come dressed in wedding attire. I, on the other hand, looked like a clown going to entertain children at a birthday party. Dian's frantic call made me move faster with my mind moving even more slowly as I prepared to walk out the door with the green grocery bag instead of the bag with the white wine I had bought to bribe her family into accepting me.

My pink trousers started to flash and vibrate just as I began emptying the bag of groceries from which two notebooks emerged. As I panicked looking at messages and calls from Dian demanding I reach there immediately, my apprehension increased as five stamps of LSD fell out from between the pages of the notebooks. I was a step outside my house, with the door open and five stamps of hallucinogens scattered outside my door. I immediately leaped to pick them up. My heart beating faster, I clumsily... I clumsily picked up the strips just before my landlady and neighbour opened the door.

'Good evening, dear, what are you doing bent over the floor?' her timid voice was perfectly suited to her petite image as she stood shyly behind her veil.

'Hi sister. Oh, it's nothing. I'm going to my girlfriend's for dinner. I'll see you later,' unblinking, I held tightly to my LSD-filled pocket.

'God bless you, dear,' her tone filled with pity; she smiled at me, hinting she sensed my anxiety. A blessing is what I needed and for a Hindu atheist, I too prayed nervously that the Hindu and Catholic gods would instill confidence in me.

London is a busy city with high rise buildings eclipsing one another, casting odd shadows over people who aspire to live on the top floor of these buildings. Each pedestrian has his own story and this can be read in the way they walk. There are the sprinters, the overly eager citizens who always want to be first. These are the same people who would wake up hours ahead of time to reach a theme park, just to go through each ride enough times for the adrenaline rush to subside. Then there are the trotters. These are the hopeless wanderers who are either lost or carefree; they walk slowly enough for a tortoise to win against them. Lastly, we have the confused souls, who run five steps and then take to trotting nervously because they are on their way to a destination that demands much more of them then they can offer. I fit into the last category. I am an epitome of this section of disoriented strollers.

As I ran across the city filled with red buses and black cabs, I got closer to a disorderly line of stationary travellers who were all getting pushed into a tunnel. Sucked into the London Underground which could be thought of as a grey city in itself during rush hour, we all stand like robots staring into a black tunnel waiting for a light to guide us to our destination. All in sync with the other, no glances are shared despite the absurd way I am dressed. I look like a man who found it hard to part ways with his childhood jumper as it hugged me in such a way so as to show that I was far above a low body fat percentage.

The boards hanging from cobwebbed metallic stands showed the arrival time for our train and with each minute, every pedestrian adopted a stance like an Olympic sprinter.

Wary of carrying LSD in my pockets, my paranoia didn't allow me to leave them at the flat just in case some petty burglar broke in. Like a used bottle I was crushed to the side against a railing. My fellow passengers thought it was an act of chivalry; in reality I was fidgety enough to have run the whole way.

Men and women in suits, boys in caps covered with hoods and couples holding hands. This train had enough stories to create a series of novels about every life. The Underground was the one destination where a person could take a time out from the world as there was no connectivity or signal to disturb our deep thoughts. The train moved at rapid speed like my thoughts. Just as the darkness from either sides was snuffled out by the streetlights that emerged as the train moved over ground, civilization caught up and my phone started to buzz viciously; it was flashing the name of the reason that my ceiling and ears were being wrecked every day.

'Hello, yeah. I can barely hear you. Dimitrov, give me a second and I'll call you back.' A crackling Russian voice muttered on the other end as my phone disconnected, deciding that I would have to stay off it.

As we moved back over ground, my phone lit up like the street lights, flashing the name of the 28-year-old Russian.

'I told you I was calling. Why can't you Russians ever learn to cooperate!' my exhilaration now turned into anger. It helped me vent my nervousness.

'Did you hire a new guy to deliver your stuff? I got five stamps off some fashion guru nutter,' holding onto my pocket as I protected its contents, I completed my sentence just in time to hear a loud, concerned reply.

'You got a new dealer! I didn't send anyone. You fucking sucka! I left two tabs of acid under your apartment door just this morning. You better pay me!' he sounded disheartened at the thought that I had betrayed him.

'I have no idea who this guy is but he charged practically nothing for the amount I have; and I was home the entire morning, I didn't receive anything. I live a floor below you! Stop being so doped up all the time!' my conversation was attracting more attention than was necessary as those around me shuffled, curious.

'I dropped it off at yours sucka. 102! 102! Right where you live, you cheat!' he repeated his Russian abuse. He sounded more offended than a drug dealer should be at his client.

'I stay in 101, right below you! You just delivered acid to a nun, you idiot! She's going to be in the confession for a week because of this. Make the drop to me personally next time!

Don't go distributing acid like it's the Bible, you fool!' I was peeved at his stupidity and unprofessional attitude and my request attracted even more concerned attention and glares.

'Anyway, I'm off now and you owe me ninety quid for my ceiling. You need to take it easy on your floor, you're breaking my ceiling with each attempt at screwing your way into this country,' my irritated voice was laced with jealousy at the drug dealer who had more grass in his head than brain cells and was definitely getting more action than I was.

I disconnected the call just in time to prepare myself for the dinner like a fighter on his way to the boxing ring. A jaded announcement made all us commuters aware that we had reached Oxford Circus Station. I was welcomed by a text from Dian that did not seem peaceful in the least.

'*You're late! If you didn't want this dinner, you didn't have to come. You don't celebrate Christmas, so you shouldn't try to ruin it for us.*'

I was the definition of a whipped boyfriend and this time the whip hit me hard enough to get me to run the next mile, completely ignoring the cold winds that shrivelled the part of my body in her hands.

I stood outside the door, my hands shivered with nervousness, my fingers moving closer to the doorbell. Like a prospective employee going into a final round of interview, I rehearsed my handshake and greeting. Too formal and I would seem pretentious. Too familiar and I would seem over-eager. I looked at the watch with the brown leather strap that pulsated quicker each time my pulse raced with anxiety. I found I was on time. For Indian Standard Time that was blasphemous. Even though I was from a country where I had been taught that the later you reach the more importance you get, I was an eager beaver as per the western lingo I desperately hoped to adopt.

Out of all of Dian's family, I had never had the chance to meet Uncle Jon. But I knew enough about him to call him my Uncle. He was the family's goose that laid the golden egg and quite literally so, with his multi-million pound poultry business. He was a man who didn't care whether the chicken came first or the egg, as long as they both came. He was suave and in his forties. His mental age seemed to decrease each year as if to keep up with the times. Living in a three bedroom flat in central London, his son, Timothy, was Uncle Jon's and the family's pride. No one knew who the mother was but no one questioned Uncle Jon either. Like a hen warming her eggs, he protected Timothy.

Looking like a Christmas carol singer who was raising funds for better clothes, I pressed the doorbell which rang inside the overpriced mansion.

'Hi mate, you all right? Nice to finally meet you, fella!' a voice deep enough to perform in London musicals greeted me. I stared directly at a Christmas tree adorned tie; it was worn by a man tall enough for my neck to hurt while looking at him.

Prepared and confident I put my hand out firmly to shake his, but instead poked his blazer; my hand was caught in a hug I was not prepared for. The warmth from his greeting felt even more heated to my hand that was caught in between both our sloppy stomachs.

'Sorry, I think I am late,' I stuttered nervously. I stepped into his brightly lit house that resembled an antique museum with artifacts that radiated wealth and success. As I retracted my forearm, which now smelt of his costly perfume, and my knockoff *'Gussi'* I walked avoiding his priceless carpets.

'You're creepily early, Koonal,' his voice echoed as it reached me below.

'That's our gem, Timothy.' He gestured to a child with legs longer than mine and a small upper body that seemed like it was eagerly waiting to grow in proportion to his legs. He was resting against a rocking chair while playing with action figures that were being flung across the room.

I was often told that if a family favourite takes to the boyfriend then the family too accepts you with open arms. So I went with mine open wide to greet him in the same manner as I had been welcomed a few seconds ago. But my attempt was in vain. Crouched awkwardly, I wrapped my arms as much as I could around the 4-year-old but he didn't reciprocate. He was holding onto the action figures. He was straight faced; his arms caught tightly between my legs as he shuffled out, giving a grunt of frustration. Uncle Jon glared in concern as he saw his child struggle past the arms of an overly eager Indian man. The awkwardness was enough to heat up the room quicker than the several heaters in the periphery alongside the walls filled with paintings.

'Where is Dian?' I asked, embarrassed as I let go off the uninterested child.

'Check you out getting eager without her,' with each sentence his southern accent seemed to get stronger.

'I thought I could hear an Indian man rattle on about some discounts,' a sober voice reached the room in which the three of us were. Dian walked in looking more beautiful than the last time I had seen her. Or this might have been the sexual frustration that made her look more beautiful. Her timid voice was deceiving. Her wavy hair bounced behind her back as she walked past me to acknowledge her nephew who was sitting like a pet tied by a leash.

'Uncle Jon, Mom and Dad said they're going to be reaching a bit late. Apparently the Piccadilly Line has been stalled,' I stood in the middle of the room feeling invisible with the hope of being involved in the conversation.

'These strikes I tell you, they never seem to end!' The irony—this was a man whose nightwear would cost more than my wardrobe—brought a grin to my face. I was certain the strike had no impact on his life. As long as the chicken could fly a short distance, he'd still be hatching golden eggs.

'This isn't because of a strike. Apparently some people heard a drug deal happening during rush hour. Do you know anything about it, Kunal?' her question seemed more like an accusation, causing me to hold on to my pockets tight.

'No, why would I?' feeling guilty despite being honest, I was close enough to popping a stamp of LSD myself just to calm my nerves.

'We have enough time to get some pesto from M&S then, dear,' the change in conversation made me take an instant liking towards Uncle Jon. From being close enough to tearing up under pressure, I was now confident enough to carry off the outfit that made me look like a mannequin at a fancy dress store.

I had been in the room for over five minutes and away from Timothy; we were all standing. Having not being asked to sit, I assumed one of the two things. Either, there was no formality between us and I had been accepted by the family or I should have gotten the hint and seen myself out. As I calculated and weighed each possibility, I felt a pull on my jumper. Coming up to just below my shoulder, Timothy looked at me straight faced. He kept jabbing me and reminding me of the extra fat. If only they knew it was a sign of prosperity back in India, I would have been asked to sit down much before. As his tugs became more vicious, I kept hoping he would tear the godawful jumper.

'Look at you two little ones taking a liking to each other,' Uncle Jon scoffed as he picked up his branded brown overcoat. I had heard of L, XL and XXL in sizes but this made them all look like an S. The size just bigger than my XS.

'Why don't you take a coat; you probably aren't used to this weather. Take our Timmy's coat. It might be a size bigger.' He sneered hyena-like as he nudged Dian like he was a teenager trying to get an audience to appreciate his forced humour. I had seen newcomers try and fit into a community by pretending to be someone they weren't. Non-smokers holding a cigarette in their hand enough to leave a mark between their fingers, just to fit in around strangers they could befriend. But Uncle Jon's tactic of offending to fit in was as contradictory as cheating on someone just to express how much you love them. The room I seated myself comfortably in was filled with several chairs. All of them had their own unconventional style, some with the arms longer than the legs, whereas others with a backrest small enough to be called a bicycle seat, yet Timothy chose to sit on my lap. Luckily for my genitals, which were turning blue from his overgrown body, his weight (like his upper body) was not proportionate to his height. As he continued to tug on my pockets, each time he was bored playing with his action figures, I kept hoping one of the toys would come to life and give him an occasional punch.

I was strong enough to push him off me but I was not keen on being associated with a child who didn't reciprocate my hug. I tried pushing him off while playfully lifting my knees. As Timothy bounced on my knee like an adult on a baby trampoline, Uncle Jon did not see the humour and fun from behind me, as his child kept grunting every time he was launched into the air.

'Timothy, get off! Let's go son and you too, Koonal,' he instructed somewhat frightened by the sight that presented a different picture to the possessive father. We both stood up immediately.

'I'm going to stay in, actually. Do you mind making some tomato puree instead, Uncle Jon?' Dian finally broke her silence as she held her head in her hands looking like a boxer who had been knocked out. Her mumble was audible enough to suggest that she was tired. As a paranoid boyfriend, I was hoping it wasn't me she was tired of.

'You should get yourself checked dear, you've been awfully pale ever since you came here. Anyway, Koonal, you know where everything is; why don't you and Timmy play a game and I'll be in the kitchen.' When he left, the lack of his large frame made more space in the room as I was provided with a responsibility as large enough as the delegator.

I tried implying I'd join Dian and have some much longed for alone time, but my forced romanticism was left hanging. Now it was just me, Timothy and the strange sculptures that reminded me of Greek mythology.

Coming from a large extended family, I was used to taking care of younger cousins and their friends and at times even toddlers, when we didn't know which cousin's friends they belonged to. I was a professional babysitter by experience but all that entailed was making sure they stayed asleep and didn't eat what they shit. Left in a room full of antiques, I had been made responsible for a child who was more valuable than all of them combined. He proceeded to tug on my trouser pockets with more energy than a 4-year-old should have. I tried several strategies to assert my superiority. For one, I was a university student and a primary school child could not outsmart me. I eventually gave in to his constant pleas and handed my phone to him to finally establish peace so I could prepare myself for the dinner.

I finally had a few genuine laughs while watching Family Guy, as I noted the resemblance between the child on the show and the one I had to tend to. The on screen one always looked high as I watched Timothy holding my phone in one hand and the reasons for my worry in the other. I dug deep into each pocket, searching like a miner digging for diamonds. But my worry came true as Timothy sat on the floor waving the five acid stamps in his hands like they were balloons from a fair. I had felt panic before but never had such torment made me sweat profusely in the cold. I stretched my hand forward to take the hallucinogens but my relentless effort was interpreted as a game causing him to dodge and run around the room in circles. All my years of playing kabaddi in school were being tested with each lunge. His actions and speed were astonishing for his age and he outwitted me. Just as he realized he was holding something that controls our daily lives, he threw it towards a sculpture of a naked disc thrower. I jumped reflexively to protect my phone. I lay face up looking at a waxed sculpture's genitals. This is when Timothy popped two stamps in his mouth; his expression immediately becoming sour and sullen.

There are certain times in life when our actions lead the way to our future. This was one of those tests. I had to tend to a child who would soon start visualizing many such ways and everything else his mind could concoct. His straight faced expression was intermittently replaced by absurd expressions, his mouth unable to figure out the dry sandpaper texture of the stamps.

'What have you two boys been up to?' Uncle Jon walked in wearing an apron in addition to his attire forty minutes into the trip which would be bad for the two of us.

'*Next Two and a Half Men only on Channel 4,*' the bright television occupied my terrified thoughts and Timothy was intrigued by each flashing light on the screen.

'I'd love a drink inside of me,' an energized voice interrupted my thoughts as Dian walked in, seeming more cheerful than I had seen her in a month. She sat down by my side.

'Sure, dear. I could do with a beer myself and a coke for you, Koonal?'

'I'd have a pint, as well, please.' I could have finished a keg in the state I was in. I tried calming Timothy who was going around walking and waving his hands in the air.

'A what?' Uncle Jon seemed shocked.

'He'll have a glass of champagne with me,' Dian took the liberty of voicing my unsaid thoughts.

'But you can't drink. You're a Hindu, innit?'

'I drink,' ignoring his ignorance, I was close enough to sharing the acid trip with his son and joining a world far away from the hazy one Uncle Jon lived in.

'Well, blimey! I learn something new every day.' As he handed us each a drink, I could not wait for the polite glass clinking and quenching my paranoia.

'Dear, how's the headache? Do you need any Paracetamol? Koonal, recommend something.'

Dian laughed reaffirming that the hyena-like trait was genetic within the Turner family. 'He's hopeless; he'd try and save a fish from downing. And he's studying Economics with me, so I'd rather take Timmy's medical advice,' she completed the sentence by stroking the young boy's head, as he sat sweating from all the thoughts that were playing in his head.

'You must be one of the rare few from your country, wouldn't you?' Uncle Jon's lack of cultural awareness reminded me of someone from the start of the nineteenth century brought to 2016. I on the other hand, wanted to go back in time, even if it were to the nineteenth century, just to prevent Timothy from making random sounds like a wasp as he dragged his feet backwards performing a failed moonwalk. Uncle Jon and I both analysed each of his strange movements, his neck moving around slower each time making us feel like time had itself slowed down. Lost in my own world, calculating the consequences of this unaccounted, for mishap, I studied Timothy as he glided around, lost in his own world.

A sound of chapped lips and a clicking of the tongue started to hint at the occurrence of odd behaviour from Timothy; that was luckily interrupted as Dian choked on her drink, gasping for fresh air.

'Oh my god! A ring! A ring! He proposed to me!' she screamed joyfully, holding up a champagne-soaked ring.

I sat impassive in a state of shock, unaware of the proposal while Timothy ran out of the room oblivious to his surroundings.

'This calls for a bottle of champagne!' Uncle Jon blithely stood up to get a bottle, unaware of the confusion of the moment, while Dian was filled with glee, taking pictures of her newly accessorized finger.

As my impromptu fiancée and I were left in the room, my pent-up concern was going to turn into a rapid fire of questions. Just then Timothy entered, running in circles around me like a shark circling its prey. Patience is the power to endure everything that is around you but like everything, even tolerance has its limits and mine had reached the breaking point. Just as I was about to shove Timothy aside, I found a wet stick in his mouth.

'What the hell is this?' I gestured to the pregnancy test, close to collapsing from the overdose of absurd events.

'That's not mine, baby,' the words that flew out of Dian's mouth were sweeter than I had ever heard.

'I'm pretty sure Uncle Jon won't be needing this either.' Throwing the positive test to the side I downed the remainder of the champagne as a celebration of my approaching insanity.

'We're having a...' she held me close as I interrupted.

'No, we're not.'

'You're going to be...' she stroked my face as I shivered, feeling a mix of several emotions.

'I'm going to have a panic attack.' Downing the remainder of the drink, my body started to calm down from the effect of the bubbly; my brain felt overworked.

'I was going to surprise you; we're having a baby!' she hugged me in excitement as I tried pinching myself to wake up from this nightmare.

'How is that even possible? We haven't had sex in ages! Ages! You and I both know I didn't put that ring in there and...' I ranted.

'This must be from that day when...' she continued to justify.

'From when? My forearms are like bricks! We haven't had sex in a month!' I gestured in frustration showing off my arms, which were veined enough to act like evidence.

'Baby, this is from when we did and each time your floor would crack...'

Like Sherlock solving a case and a scientist discovering a planet, I had solved the puzzle.

'You and Dimitrov! You're the one who is cracking my ceiling? It's you who shrieks like a dying owl!' I was frozen, satisfied to have solved this dilemma I was being roped into. Uncle Jon walked in with two bottles of champagne which were big enough to be called his two children.

'What have I missed out on you two lovebirds?' his desperation to be young made me explode.

'Well, for starters, your daughter is screwing each BRIC country over worse than their government does!'

'There is a child here, Koonal,' he covered Timothy's ears as the acid tripper kept foxtrotting on the spot, high as a kite.

'Oh your precious one isn't so pure. He just popped two stamps of acid; so good luck handling him for the next sixteen hours!' I didn't know the exact feeling of nirvana but if it was absolute relief and the feeling of freedom, then I had reached the ultimate bliss.

Having been influenced by a country driven by Bollywood movies, all I needed now was a song and a few backup dancers to escort me out of the door, as I went towards it.

'Koonal darling!' her voice, sounding needy and desperate. Her agitated voice was like a symphony to my ears.

'It's Kunal, not Koonal! Well, how about you learn how to say Dimitrov because you don't want to piss a Russian off!'

Dinner with the Turners (Script)

The play is set in London in 2016.

Characters

Kunal: A 20-year-old Indian student studying economics at the London School of Economics. He is in his third year of college. He is originally from Delhi. As of a month ago, he lives in a small one bedroom apartment. The apartment is rundown and his ceiling has been cracking in every other day with plaster falling on his untidy carpeted floor for three weeks. He cannot wait to move out of his apartment. He is well-versed about the lifestyle in England where he has spent nearly three years in a steady relationship with Dian, whom he met through his course in the first year. The quieter of the two in the relationship and easily dominated. Comparatively short compared to Dian who has a tall frame and is yet considered to be short in a family where the average height is six foot.

Dian Turner: A 19-year-old from West London, she was born and brought up in Chiswick. Studying economics in the same year and university as Kunal, she has no career ambitions. A control freak, especially when it comes to Kunal, she thinks of him as a child. Despite coming from a fairly liberal household which is accepting of her relationships, her family is forced to accept Kunal, her first Indian boyfriend. Rather loud, she hates silences around her and loves being the centre of attention at any conversation.

Timothy: Uncle Jon's 3-year-old son, who is considerably tall for his age. This is something that makes the Turner family very happy. The pride of the family as he is the newest member, he is taken around at all gatherings and parties like a prized possession. Timothy is a bratty child, who gets away with all of his bad behaviour.

Uncle Jon: Dian's uncle, who is extremely well off and lives in a bachelor pad in central London, on Oxford Street. Very possessive about his son, Timothy. He is extremely tall and pretends to be rather suave though he is actually a complete show off.

Drug dealer: An aspiring designer, he is a 24-year-old who is keen to work with big labels on London's high street but is caught up in the drug dealing business, which provides him with regular funds. His family is originally from Pakistan, but he was born and raised in East London. A dealer around the Central Zone 1 regions of London, he aspires to deal drugs to big celebrities or designers with the aim of working with them. Currently his clients are mostly around the Elephant and Castle and Embankment area, predominantly students who pay him measly amounts for their highs.

Dimitrov (Implied Character): Russian, 28-years-old, looking for a job or a reason to stay in England, particularly London. He is a drug dealer and deals to Kunal, as well as stays on the floor above him.

Khan Saab (Implied Character): A local shop owner. He migrated from Karachi as a 21-year-old, thirty years ago. His shop is situated near a Tesco's supermarket that is open 24×7, which poses a major disadvantage to him as it diverts a large percentage of his customers away to the well-equipped convenience store. Khan Saab has been supplying Kunal with his weekly supply of vegetables ever since Kunal moved into his apartment.

Note

'...' at the end of a line signals an interruption.

'...' within a line signals a short pause.

Scene 1

6.00 p.m. in a claustrophobic student accommodation which is occupied by Kunal. The thin wall behind his bed is filled with personal pictures of himself, predominantly with Dian, along with a couple of selfies of Dian. There is a calendar around these pictures with dates crossed out until the current date, 18 December.

A single bed is in front of the wall of pictures. The bed is slightly smaller than a regular single bed and is rickety. There are several CD covers strewn across the bed, a few clothes including a red pair of trousers along with a book on 'Economics For Dummies' on top of which lies a voice recorder.

A small plastic table is placed very close to the bed on top of which is a small CD player, a magazine on designer clothes and a bowl of cereal in warm milk with a box of cereal kept next to it. The cereal is similar to cornflakes but is a knockoff version of Kellogg's.

There are clothes scattered and piled untidily near his bed, only a few folded. Four hangers are hung on a washing line with only one of them with a sports jacket hanging on it.

The scene opens with Kunal in his boxers; he has just come out of the shower, standing in front of the table. He is wearing a pink shirt and looking at a magazine that is on the table. 'All Star' by Smash Mouth is playing while he tries to sing along. The song continuously gets stuck on, 'Shape of an L on her forehead', as his CD player isn't working well. Plaster from his ceiling falls on him and his cereal bowl. Faint moans can be heard from above. He wipes the bowl in disgust as this has been a common occurrence for the past three weeks. He takes a bite of the soggy cornflakes; they are the texture he absolutely despises. He picks up a pair of red trousers that are on his bed and puts them on and tucks his shirt in like in the magazine. There is a knock on the door, which is situated very close to the bed. As he analyses his look by looking himself up and down (there is no mirror) he walks towards the door. The knocking is much louder this time. As he opens the door, a bit of plaster falls again at the same time as the faint moaning.

The music plays faintly again on its own to his surprise. It gets stuck again on 'Shape of an L on her forehead.'

As he opens the door, a man can be seen. He is fashionably dressed with sunglasses on top of his head and rings on three fingers on either hand. The man is carrying two bags, out of which one is a brown leather sling bag, slung around his right shoulder, and the other is a big green plastic packet dangling over his left arm.

Kunal opens the door and starts searching for money on an untidy table stuck adjacent to the door.

Dealer: You need to open up quicker, my friend. I don't got all day for you.

Kunal doesn't acknowledge him, nor does he look at him but starts collecting coins and a note in his hand from the table which is crowded with ties, cups and used tissues.

Dealer: What the hell are you dressed as blood...pink with red! Are you dressing up as a fucking chewing gum or what?

Kunal has now stacked up quite a few coins and small notes in his hand and begins counting them while leaning on the table.

Dealer: Any how, who am I to style you? Here's your stuff... money now, quick. I have places to be for those who need me. *(He sniggers as he rhymes the last bit, and nods so his glasses fall over his eyes without him having to use his hands)*

Kunal now looks up to the dealer as he hands over the money while taking the packet the latter offers.

Kunal: Are you new at the shop? Khan Saab never mentioned you...

Dealer: Watchu on 'bout, blood? You already high, mate?

Kunal: He never mentioned he was hiring! You got hired? I didn't! Are you getting paid for this?

Dealer: 'Course I get paid. Who else do you think grows your greens on the farm, eh? Bud, you seem stocked up already, ha!

Kunal: Huh? I'll speak to him later bout this.

The dealer starts to stroke and press his clothes as he begins to walk off.

Kunal: Wait....did you say something about my combination? Does it not match?

Dealer: Yeah, lose the frown. Oh and cheers for the extra mullah. Let's toke sometime soon. *(Gestures with his finger)*

Kunal: I...uh...don't do drugs.

Dealer: Yeah…and I'm not a drug dealer. *(He whispers the last bit)*

Kunal closes the door and quickly starts unbuttoning his shirt as he starts scouting for his blazer that is not there.

Kunal: Where is it? Where…oh fucking Anthony! These goras don't wear their own clothes or what!

Picks up his phone to call Anthony.

Kunal: Yeah, Anto, where's my blazer? *(Phone starts to beep as Dian starts to call)* I'm calling you back, wait, calling in a sec… *(Answers Dian's call)* Hi babe! Wait, what? Why are you yelling? I can't understand…no I didn't forget to call before leaving, I haven't left. Wait, what, why're you getting hysterical, we're meeting in an hour and a half… I'll be there twenty minutes before that. It only takes twenty-five minutes from Central Line. What do you mean we meet in forty? It's… *(Checks his watch)* Fuck! My watch is stuck! This fucking watch is absolute shit! No, you're not, babe! The watch! The watch, not you! Why would you be shit? Yes…yes, you got the watch…but you didn't make it, na. Anyway, I'm leaving now. I just need to change. Apparently Khan Saab's guy… Khan Saab, you've met Khan Saab. The vendor near the Tesco right under mine. Yeah, anyway he gave some fashion guru nutter a job and not me! Yes, him… the one with the pubescent beard…Yeah, I'll change…wait I can't wear that jumper, it's too small now. Yes, I know it's festive but I'm sure your mum will understand if I don't wear it. Fine, I'll wear it. *(Kunal is holding up a small red Christmas jumper that was lying on his pile of clothes)* Wait, and the scarf? But it's pink. Apparently red and pink don't match. *(He holds up the red Christmas jumper and pink scarf)* Yes, I've left, seriously. *(He rushes to his bed and picks up the voice recorder and plays the*

sound of traffic) Anyway getting to the station now, love you...
bye... *(Dian cuts the call while he's saying bye)*

Kunal now starts to rush around putting on the red jumper and is skeptical about the pink scarf which he finds extremely itchy and ends up carrying around his arm. He quickly changes from his red trousers into blue jeans and thinks about flipping through the magazine but chooses against it.

Just as he is about to leave, his phone rings.

Kunal: Haanji, Khan Saab, walaikum assalam...nahi saamaan toh abhi aaya hai...haanji...nahin kya aapne koi naya banda rakha hai kya? Khan ji, sach mein aur meine extra paise bhi de diye. Woh agle hafte ke hisab mein set kar dena. *(He picks up the green packet he was given and looks into it and starts taking out two three notebooks.)* Yeh toh kitaabe hain. *(A few pieces of paper fall out as he realizes these are acid stamps)* Mein aapko baad mein phone karta hoon...haanji...nahi baad mein!

Kunal starts to panic. His phone starts to ring. It's Dian who is calling again. He puts the stamps of acid in his right pocket along with his phone and walks out of the door in a hurry.

Scene 2

The scene opens with Kunal in the London Underground, wearing a tight Christmas jumper and holding a scarf in his hand. He has white chalk powder on his right shoulder and back that has fallen on him from his wrecked ceiling. He is standing with earphones plugged in his ears, listening to 'All Star' by Smash Mouth. The song keeps getting stuck on 'Shape of an L on her forehead'. His phone starts to ring; he takes out the earphones and puts the phone to his ear.

Tube Announcement: Welcome to the Central Line to Ealing Broadway, next station is Tottenham Court Road.

Kunal: No, I can't talk right now. Yeah, I can...I can barely hear you. Hello...hello... *(People on the tube are staring at him)* Dimitrov, give me a second man, I'm going over ground soon. Yeah wait, wait, I'm losing signal. *(His phone loses connection)*

The train is now over ground.

Tube Announcement: Tottenham Court Road, doors will open on the left, please mind the gap. This is the Central Line to Ealing Broadway.

He puts his earphones back on and keeps checking his pockets carefully to be sure nothing has fallen out. 'All Star' plays again and gets stuck in the same place.

His phone starts to ring again. He takes his earphones out and answers.

Kunal: I told you I was calling you! Why can't you Russians ever learn to cooperate, huh? No, I haven't tried it yet...I'm sure it's prime quality kush but I need it with me to smoke it now, don't I? No I haven't gotten it! No...I haven't! Wait...102, did you say 102? I'm in 101 you fucktard, I live right below you! Since when, since when! Are you always high? What kind of a dealer slips an ounce of weed under a door! You've dealt a nun a bag of grass; she's probably going to be in confession for a week because of you! Make the drop to me; don't go distributing ganja like the Bible, you fool. Oi...Dimitrov I can hardly hear you, man. How does it matter to you where I'm off to? *(A woman sitting gets scared and moves away, fiddling and typing on her phone)* I'll pay you along with next week's. No, I'm not going to run away! I live below you, you fuck-face! You need to stop getting high on your supply bud; you've got more grass in your head than cells. Yeah, we'll boom one tomorrow. This time make the drop to me! What do you mean you don't do pot? We've toked together…yes we have. No I'm not a narc you bag of weed! Oh and you need to get a hold on your clientele… I had some LV bummer give me five stamps of acid for no reason. No I don't know who it was. Right…I'm off. Oh wait, Dimitrov. Hello! Hello! Yeah, you owe me sixty quid for my ceiling. What do you mean what ceiling? If you put as much time into thinking as you do into screwing you might actually end up getting a job to stay here. Yeah, anyway, you need to take it easy on your floor; it's hurting my ceiling and my ears! It's not my fault you have bowling balls for nuts!

The other half of the stage is now visible to the audience, where we can see Uncle Jon and Timothy. They are in a nicely done up home, filled with paintings that surround a rectangular table with candles and fine cutlery on it. Timothy is sketching and constantly pestering Uncle Jon who is giving him a lot of attention. Uncle Jon is trying to set the dinner table at the same time. He is in a suit, adding ornaments around his house. The above action continues until Kunal reaches the door.

Tube Announcement: This is Oxford Circus station… *(Kunal walks out of the train as his phone rings)*

Kunal: Hi babe. I'm literally ten minutes off, so I'm going to leg it to you now… Yes, I am wearing the jumper. Yes, and the scarf. *(Puts the crumpled scarf around his neck)* Please tell everyone I'll be there very soon. *(Starts to run).* Love you, bye. *(The phone is disconnected as he's saying bye)*

'All Star' plays in the background and it stops at the line 'Shape of an L on her forehead' as Kunal rings the doorbell. The door is centre stage, dividing the stage in half.

Kunal: Hi! *(Goes for a handshake while Uncle Jon goes in for a big hug)*

Uncle Jon: O'right, good to finally meet you fella...

Kunal: *(Mid-hug)* Sorry I'm late...

Uncle Jon: You're creepily early, Koonal...the dinner isn't till half past seven, mate.

Kunal: Oh...

Kunal approaches Timothy as Jon is speaking to him and gives him a hug as he gathers that's how the Turners like to greet. The hug is not reciprocated; instead Timothy shrugs him off which makes Uncle Jon glare at Kunal.

Kunal: Where's Dian?

Uncle Jon: Check you out getting all fidgety without her, eh? *(Winks at him)* She's being a gem helping me with dinner...

Dian walks in from the wings.

Dian: I thought I could hear a little Indian man rattle on about some discounts.

Uncle Jon laughs.

Kunal smiles, happy to see her, but is ignored as Dian walks past him to Timothy.

Dian: *(To Kunal as she walks past him)* Wow, you've gained holiday fat before the holidays.

Kunal: I told you, it's tight.

Dian: Uncle Jon, Mum and Dad just called. They said the two of them and Sara are stuck because Central Line has been stalled.

Uncle Jon: These strikes never seem to end, now, do they?

Dian: It's not that, apparently some woman heard a drug deal being settled on her way to Oxford Street.

Kunal checks his pockets.

Dian: *(To Kunal)* You heard anything 'bout that?

Kunal: No...why would I?

Uncle Jon: So Koonal...how did you get my sweet niece to fall into your trap...

Kunal: Sorry, what...

Uncle Jon: *(Speaks slowly and his actions are condescending)* How did you two get together?

Dian is texting on her phone, not bothered about the conversation.

Kunal: Oh, hah! *(Looks at Dian who is still glued to her phone)* We met in first year in my dorm room...

Uncle Jon: Jesus, Koonal! Spare me the details, please. I said how did you meet not...

Kunal: Oh gosh...No, no, nothing like that! We met because Dian and my roommate at the time were close friends; then he had to go back to India...

Uncle Jon: Ah, of course...let me guess, illegal immigrant, got deported and...?

Kunal: No…he went back for business; his family is into the hotelier business…

Uncle Jon: I think you picked the wrong Indian eh, D. *(Dian looks up and acknowledges them with half a smile then goes back to her phone)*

Kunal: Ha ha! It's funny you say that because the first thing I told Dian was that my roommate, Raghav, and I were business partners.

Dian sighs, looking bored.

Kunal: Anyway, he moved back and since then I couldn't afford these student accommodations. They're so expensive you know!

Uncle Jon: Not a 'very good price'. *(Tries and imitates an Indian accent and laughs. Dian acknowledges this time with more intent)*

Timothy is now standing next to Kunal tugging on his jumper for no reason.

Uncle Jon: Look at you two taking a liking to each other. Isn't our Timmy an absolute joy?

Kunal nods nervously.

Dian: Right, we have time to pick up pasta sauce from M&S then.

Uncle Jon: Yeah, I'll get myself a coat and let's all head…you can get our Timmy's coat for yourself if you like; it might be a size too big? *(Gestures to Kunal)*

Uncle Jon and Dian laugh.

Dian's phone buzzes and it looks like she starts feeling a bit unwell and queasy.

Dian: I've changed my mind actually…I'm going to take a nap. Uncle Jon do you mind making some pesto sauce instead?

Uncle Jon: Sure dear, you need to get yourself checked. You've been awfully pale all day.

Dian nods and walks offstage.

Uncle Jon: I'm going to be right here if you need me. Take care of our Timmy.

Kunal: Yes, definitely.

Uncle Jon: You're big enough…well, old enough to.

Uncle Jon walks offstage.

Kunal and Timothy now stare at each other as Timothy keeps tugging at his trousers and doesn't speak.

Kunal: Hello Timmy…what would you like to do?

Timothy keeps tugging at and pinching him.

Kunal: Ow…fuc…

Timmy stares at him in shock, still tugging, as Kunal pauses halfway through swearing.

Kunal gives him his phone. The acid strips also fall out. Kunal doesn't realize this.

Kunal is sitting idle and turns on the television, as an episode of Family Guy begins. In the background, one can hear Dian talking on the phone.

Dian: Yeah, I checked again…I'm sure. I'm not retarded, I can read signs. What do you mean it can't be? It is…wait, hello…hello…

Kunal now realizes Timothy is playing with the acid stamps, while he is sitting on his lap watching the show.

Kunal: *(Whispers as he tries to take the strips in exchange for the TV remote)* Timothy, here boy, take this…please just take this and give those to me.

Timothy starts frantically waving the strips. Kunal tries snatching the strips away as Timothy throws his phone on the ground in protest. Kunal reflexively jumps to get his phone and dives, trying to catch it. In the process he manages to get a hold of three strips. He sees Timothy now sitting on the chair holding two strips of the LSD and teasing him by waving them. Kunal stretches in an attempt to snatch them but doesn't succeed. Timothy eats both the strips.

Kunal: *(He mouths)* Oh fuck.

Kunal starts to panic as Timothy makes weird faces because of the bitter taste. He goes back to playing with Kunal's phone as Kunal sits, nervously watching the show.

The end of Family Guy plays as a voice on the TV announces, 'Next on Channel 4, watch Two and Half Men'.

Uncle Jon comes in.

Uncle Jon: How have you two boys bonded?

Timothy is now wandering all over the stage, quietly making strange movements in slow motion.

Kunal: We were fine…watched an episode of *Family Guy*.

Uncle Jon: He's three, Koonal! He can't be watching shows like that!

Dian walks in looking distressed.

Uncle Jon: You alright, lovey?

Dian: Yeah, just got a mild headache.

Uncle Jon looks at Kunal.

Uncle Jon: Go on prescribe something Koonal.

Kunal: I...

Dian: He's hopeless; he'd try saving a fish from drowning.

They are now seated, with Dian at the head of the table, Kunal on her left, facing the stage.

Dian now starts stroking Kunal's leg and upper thigh under the table discreetly. Kunal is becoming aroused by this but is trying to be subtle.

Timothy who is again sitting on Kunal's lap is now staring around the room quietly.

Uncle Jon: I've never seen our Timmy so quiet; he must be really comfortable around you.

Kunal: *(Laughs nervously)* Yes, he's an absolute treat...joy.

Uncle Jon: So Koonal, how many more years till you become a doctor?

Kunal: I'm...

Dian: Haha! He could never; he's studying economics with me.

Uncle Jon: Isn't that strange! You must be one of the rare few from your country now, won't you?

Kunal: Actually...

Dian: I've had such a stressful day you know, I'd love a drink in me right now.

Uncle Jon: Well said D! I'll have a pint of lager as well and for you...a coke? *(Signals to Kunal as he gets up to get it)*

Kunal: A pint, as well, please.

Uncle Jon: A what?

Dian: We'd like two glasses of Moët. *(Points at Kunal as she mentions the champagne)*

Uncle Jon: Our man here can't be drinking...

Kunal: Why not?

Uncle Jon: Religion? You're a Hindu, innit?

Kunal: I drink...

Uncle Jon: Well, blimey...I keep learning new things.

Uncle Jon places the drink near Kunal and sits next to him, putting his arm around Kunal's shoulder.

Uncle Jon: So Koonal, tell me, man to man...what are your intentions with our lil D, eh? *(He looks down and sees that Kunal is aroused, with Timothy sitting on his lap)*

Uncle Jon: What the fu...what are you intentions with Timothy more like! *(Indicates his arousal and gets Timothy off his lap)*

Kunal: *(Laughs nervously and then realizes what Uncle Jon was implying)*....Oh my god! No...it's really not...I didn't mean to.

Uncle Jon: Right, you all are a strange lot...anyway what's this white dust on your jumper...

Kunal dusts it off with disgust.

Kunal: The lad staying above my flat has been having loud rampant *(whispers)* sex for the past month. This plaster keeps showering down on me as a reminder.

Uncle Jon: *(He whispers)* Ah, uni life, how I miss it.

Kunal: He's not a student; he's just a Russian dealer screwing his way through to stay in the country.

Timothy trots off-stage.

Uncle Jon: Right...anyway, Koonal have you eaten Italian food or will this be a first?

Dian: He...

Kunal: Yeah, I love Italian.

Dian glares at him for interrupting her.

Uncle Jon: You said Indian, yeah? I mean, who doesn't like a bit of curry, eh, D? *(Referring to Kunal as 'curry')*

Kunal: Italia...

Dian: I like to mix it up really; it can be a pain in the arse at times...if you know what I mean.

Uncle Jon: *(Laughs awkwardly)*

Dian takes a sip of her champagne and chokes on her drink because of a ring.

Dian: Oh...my god! A ring! A ring! He's proposed to me!

Kunal has no idea where this ring came from.

Dian: Oh my! I wish he'd have waited for Mum and Dad…

Uncle Jon: Well, doesn't that call for a bottle of champagne! *(Gets up to get one)*

Kunal: Wait what…

Kunal now stands up nervously and starts to gulp his drink as Timothy comes running on stage with something in his mouth. He keeps running in circles around Kunal who calms him down only to find a positive pregnancy test in his mouth.

Kunal: *(Holding the pregnancy test in his hand)* What the fuck is this!

Dian: That's not mine!

Kunal: *(Looks straight at Timothy)* I'm pretty sure your Uncle Jon doesn't need this either!

Dian: I was going to surprise you!

Kunal: Surprise me? Surprise me with what?!

Dian: We're going to…

Kunal: No, we aren't!

Dian: We're having a…

Kunal: *(Staring at the pregnancy test)* I'm having a panic attack!

Dian: We're going to have a baby!

Kunal: *(He leans on the table and looks straight at her)* You're pregnant?! But we haven't had sex in ages! Ages! Like four weeks!

Dian: *(Whispers)* Ha, yeah we have!

Kunal: You and I both know I didn't plant that ring in there and now it makes sense why you...

Dian: Ha of course we have, baby. This must be from...

Kunal: Must be from when, when could this possibly be from?

Dian: This is from that time when...

Kunal: My forearms...my forearms have been like bricks for a month! *(Stretches his arms out)*

Dian: Kunal!

Kunal: Unless my hands are connected to your ovaries, there is no way this could have happened!

Dian: This is from that night. I think it was the first of the month when your floor started to crack each time we...

Kunal: My ceiling...

Dian: Yeah...your ceiling...that's what I said, each time your ceiling...

Kunal: You said floor...you and Dimitrov! You're the one causing my ceiling to crack! It's you who screeches like a dying owl...

Uncle Jon: *(Walks up to the table with two bottles of champagne in his hands)* What have I missed out on, you two lovebirds, eh?

Kunal gets up and throws the scarf on the floor.

Kunal: Well...for starters your niece is fucking each BRIC country over worse than their government does!

Uncle Jon: What! There's a child here Koo...

Kunal: Oh yea...about him...your prized possession isn't so pure! He just popped two stamps of acid, so good luck handling him for the next sixteen hours.

Timothy is now sitting with his back towards the audience, stroking an imaginary wall.

Kunal walks off exiting the door present centre stage, as sounds from Dian's parents are audible.

Family: Koonal, darling.

Kunal: It's not Koonal! It's Kunal for fuck's sake! Anyway, no point now. How about you start learning how to say Dimitrov? You don't want to piss a Russian off!

Kunal walks through the door and plugs his earphones in, now standing on the other side of the stage from where he had entered. 'All Star' starts playing from 'Hey now you're an All Star'.

Note

When the cast is thanking the audience, they should not be standing in a line. 'All Star' keeps playing in the background faintly.

Kunal should not be wearing the Christmas jumper. He would be sipping a pint of beer on the other side of the door, standing away from Dian. She is the only one facing the audience directly and showing them her ring. Uncle Jon is looking shocked, staring and trying to take care of Timothy, who has his back to the audience, staring at a wall.

An Everlasting Travel, a Never-ending Journey

*L*ife is the biggest and most unprofitable investment we make, if we don't play it correctly. I sat on my bedroom floor surrounded by a mountain of clothes and an unused suitcase, raring to leave the city. The world is made to be travelled across. It is an insult to its splendour if the journey is not taken. We have all been travellers, from the very beginning. We travel on the inside, manoeuvring our life's journey, hoping to find ourselves sunbathing on a beach. It had been less than twenty-four hours since I had graduated from college, getting a degree I didn't want, at a university that had been forced to take me. I received congratulatory messages from well-wishers who I spoke to rarely. Their wishes made me wonder why they were lauding graduation, a common achievement. Three years of bunked classes resulted in a laminated paper that stamped the acceptance that I was now society's definition of a conventional 21-year-old. Two out of my three years of university had been spent busy with internships that would make my CV worth looking at for over six seconds. I had raised enough money to reward myself with the graduation present I wanted; travelling to India's most relaxing destination, Goa. Finally, the standard nine to five jobs which sucked my inner creativity dry helped me to take a highly anticipated gap year. While the rest of my friends got jobs to make something of themselves, I took the unconventional route to become a yearlong resident in Portugal's legacy in India. They all sent selfies of themselves wearing graduation caps whereas I went straight to makemytrip.com to confirm my booking. Within a few minutes, I had a smile on my face just like the others.

My mind continues to time travel, thinking of the past, as I stumble upon pictures of myself as a 4-year-old. The man holding the picture seems a stranger and I can now lie about myself enough for it to seem true. Lost within my own four walls, I scraped through these years with my knees on the ground and hands folded in the air, continuously praying that time would fly.

The last three years of my life had been monotonous and eventful at the same time. My parents had split up during my first year at college after they both revealed their extramarital affairs. This left me confused choosing the lesser of the evils. My brother left home to never return after his gap year and my closest companion, Bruno, passed away a few days later. His loyalty got the better of him. He had loved Akshay as though the latter was his older brother, too, and his running away changed the very energetic pug into the quietest pet, as though he was a stuffed animal. I developed immunity towards loss. Just like a frequent patient, I became numb and oblivious of the impact each fresh pain had on me. I feared loss enough to act like a stranger every time it knocked on my door. Along with my friends, who were now leaving and getting busy with their work and further studies, Ria was the only constant figure in my life. But life plans obstacles at every turn. We broke up a year ago. Over three hundred days since she has been out of the country. What made this harder was the respect and dignity with which it had come to an unexpected standstill. We both always knew this relationship would end. What hurt inside was not her leaving but the departure of someone close to me, yet again. I feared loss and it stalked me until I became the prime example of Murphy's Law. Inside, I felt defeated. I didn't know what it meant to be human and living freely was a phrase only heard in the motivational speeches I attended as regularly as though they were Sunday prayer meets. The warm air from my lungs and the constantly changing frown on my face were the only two indicators that I was still alive. Every day I rose to the rising sun and stared at its changing shades as time worked like an artist adding strokes of darker shades till the moon took over. I remember playing a board game about life when I was younger. All I had to do then was to roll the dice and sit back, watching each move lead to a better outcome. The only similarity between the board game and the game of life is that it is as unpredictable as throwing dice. I lived each day hoping it would be better than the last, but somehow hopes didn't do justice to my patience. Thinking all this while I finished packing my suitcase made it easier for me to leave. I wasn't good at saying goodbye because of the abruptness at the end of each chapter that had meant the most to me. Luckily, there were fewer goodbyes and not much left to be lost. I downloaded my boarding pass on my phone, waiting to take the cheapest flight with no return booked. The only saving grace to my sanity was the assurance that travelling the world would be something I could always have and cherish. As certain as the earth's rotation around the sun, I knew this love of mine will not ditch me as long as I had the world to travel and MakeMyTrip to serve as the travel agent. The ambiguity in my life propelled the excitement. I looked forward to my year of getting lost in the world I was only theoretically familiar with. Despite being an obstacle in the way of letting anything dear near me, I knew my passion for travelling wouldn't end. With the frequency in flights and easy access of my travel application, I had the world at my fingertips and my legs eager to walk every path.

Two and half hours after spending time amid the clouds I was welcomed by white sands, swaying palms and the sparkling water of the Arabian Sea. For the smallest state in India, the roads were smoother than silk as I glided along them to what would be my rented home in Mapusa for a year.

'Here to party, boss?' Rajesh, my driver who hailed from a village named Bastora, joked while readjusting his blue framed Aviator glasses.

The fresh breeze of India's Porto calmed my nerves. Out of all the drivers available outside the airport, fate had led me to pick Rajesh. His charismatic approach of holding the sign board *'Stairway Further Into Heaven—Rajesh Taxis'* and palm tree covered shorts matched by a subtler shirt, pulled me towards his *'Retreat Seat'* as he referred to his SUV.

'Here for a year. So that will be one on the list.' For someone from the concrete jungle of Delhi, I had loosened up enough to deem myself Goan.

'Oh, so you're here to "find yourself" then,' he said with the wisdom of a learned saint.

I confessed, breathing in the fresh air which hinted at the monsoon's arrival, 'To be honest, I'm here to lose myself.'

'That's the same thing, boss. You have to get lost in order to find.' His choice of words was like a true movie cliché, however, they became the subject to the start this journey.

'Where are the places to eat and party here?' I pondered over his words, changing the subject.

'From Anjuna all the way down to Loliem you will find everything you need, boss. This place is an encyclopaedia. We have everything for everyone.' He was like a shot of feni with the rush of excitement. His guttural voice calmed my nerves along with the hypnotic effect of Goa. We drove past hills that overlooked the vast sea which kissed the warm sand. Coconut trees stood tall bearing the thirst quenchers which were sweeter than crushed sugar, while shacks sold beverages and warm snacks for herds of travellers. A sign on a few of the clay constructions read, *'Goa is like a fridge because all you do is chill here.'* This truth became the theme for my escape, as I eagerly waited to adopt it.

We spoke nonstop during our one hour journey till we reached my one bedroom accommodation in Mapusa. The house looked artistically run down. The green walls reminded me of the trees that towered over the roof casting shadows of coconuts. The fruit filled with sweet water dangled waiting to knock against the roof when they ripened. I felt more relaxed than a yogi and I had only spent a few hours in this state. My time ahead was as bright as the morning sun, the rays of which illuminated this paradise. Rajesh introduced me to Goa like a proud owner. He spoke of the party destinations, the umpteen selections of spices and flavours that mixed together to create Goan food, along with the flea markets in Anjuna Beach held every Wednesday. As I was staying for a year I had so many options that it would take me more time to experience; soon 365 days didn't seem enough. Rajesh didn't know me but given his warmth and hospitality as we drove past silent hills in the background covered by trees, we could have been mistaken for long lost friends. Along with catering to my basic necessities, he mentioned yoga and salsa classes that were held in Mapusa itself. Neither my mind nor body was flexible. I noted his suggestions out of courtesy, but put them all the way at the end of my list.

Goa boasts of Portuguese architecture, evidently making it a suitable getaway destination for people who want to witness natural beauty. The people were the icing on top of this extravagant cake, their kindness and hospitality overflowing. All these characteristics competed with their warmth in this sunny state, making my first month fly past. I covered the streets of Baga, making each night club a hub to meet new people as the stars covered the sky. The exquisiteness of these places that stretched to Anjuna beach and Calangute was in their versatility. At night these clubs vibrated with bass and the minute a yellow light was spotted in the skies, there was serenity on the streets, with the only attraction being the aroma of Goan delicacies and speakers playing jazz. It was easy to understand why India fought with enormous perseverance to claim a state that is blessed with rich culture, mouth-watering food and impeccable aesthetics, making it a complete package.

Rajesh looked after all my chores, even teaching me the local dialect of Konkani. Soon the rice fields that surrounded the picturesque state became my home. I hired a gearless motorbike to navigate the narrow streets with the confidence of a local, knowing where each turn took me. I was well-located in Goa's largest town and every vendor knew Fridays were when I would come to restock my groceries. I experienced the true meaning of comfort. Just over a month into being disconnected from my life back home, I found a new home in Goa.

The markets were bustling with Cuban music, celebrating the end of the week. The energy in this market filled with bakers, butchers and clothes shops offered a wide selection of anything we were greedy for. At 5 p.m., this energy seemed to have increased enough to attract my attention. My 4 p.m. grocery rituals on Fridays were much quieter than the electricity that flowed within the joyful shopkeepers towards a hard working day.

I looked at my list of groceries next to the list of activities to do in Mapusa and the only one I had not ticked was at the bottom of the page. This unticked activity was the same reason the streets resembled a dance floor, making everyone's feet move gracefully. Goa brought out a side of me I wasn't aware of and this spontaneity caused me to choose to enter the four storey building from which the noise sounded more electrifying with each step I took.

I had never understood what 'two left feet' meant. I wasn't exactly skilled when it came to dancing but I imagined I'd be better than what I had got myself into. A one-off salsa session wouldn't hurt anyone but I couldn't have been more incorrect. She stood elegantly admiring us all enter taking tiny, nervous steps, as a previous session of beginners walked out covered in sweat and filled with adrenaline. The music in the room enhanced the rhythm of our bodies. She smiled making her mascaraed eyes squint, on a face softer than butter. She was like the sea on a calm night, her forehead smooth except for a few blonde wisps falling over lean shoulders. Like nursery students entering school for the first time, we were all clueless and excited. She didn't say a word, waltzing around the room handing us all a rose. Gliding across, fooling us into believing the ground was ice, her arched feet steered her fragile glasslike body. This room of fourteen contained six couples and my lone, nervous self, yet we all connected with the energy her presence radiated across the four walls. Her white dress and a tie-and-dyed scarf blended like the blue sky with the clouds. With each movement she was like the sky on a summer morning. Her movements said more about her than I could imagine saying about myself and we were all mesmerized by the comfort that loosened the muscles in our body, enabling us to smile together.

'I've introduced myself to you, you all have my name,' her words blended perfectly with the trumpets that hypnotized us into believing these too were coming from the speakers.

'As you now know, my name is Rose.' She held out the cherry red flower, raising it like it was a champagne toast, while she smiled hinting at her playful personality. Soon, there was no room for awkwardness between these walls. No indication that we were alien to one another and there wasn't any space for strangeness in this carefree environment. She didn't increase the volume but soon the music became clearer to our ears, making a sense of familiarity seep into our muscles that became attuned to the rhythm. She didn't ask for an introduction or names. 'Actions will introduce us,' she sang melodiously, complementing her every move with a twist and shuffle of her hips and feet. My body swayed two seconds slower than my brain commanded it to. Soon the awe I had felt for her ever since I had entered took charge of the movement that I was struggling with. Even a novice could have spotted my anxiousness which made the music seem strange to my ears. My feet glued to the wooden flooring ached with the adrenaline in my body acting as an adhesive clamping them together. If the visualization in my head could be projected, my dance would have introduced myself as supremely as I hoped for, but embarrassingly I resembled a restless sleeper. Each couple took cover of their partner shielding their attempts of being avid learners. I felt warmth on my cold forearms while they began to move to the rhythm instructed by her long hands. A puppet guided by her movement, she steered my arms from behind, releasing the pent-up tension that handcuffed them.

'Imagine you're a feather being guided by the wind,' her whisper tickled my ears, while I got lost in the fresh breeze that guided me.

'Thank you. Hi, I'm...' searching for words, I was interrupted by her presence.

'I'll get to know you.' Her short sentences added to the mystery and all I had known was her name. In a trance from a feeling I had forgotten about, I felt comfortable in the presence of a stranger. An hour had never felt shorter bringing the session to an end. I looked around for a schedule to pre-book another opportunity to get to know more behind the name that teased me with each of her graceful movements. Frantically searching, I was left disappointed with no results in front of me.

Certain people cross each other quick enough to be missed before we can turn our head to catch another glimpse. Rose became a mere piece of fiction in my imagination and a figment in my memory. I was angry that I had internally created a story about the future while being lost in the present we were sharing. Left with delusions of what could be, I had to concoct what had happened. Our heart has a tendency of sensing other heartbeats around it. Like a lion, it doesn't like being alone and pretends to be fierce when it is. However, this intricately constructed muscular organ is forever in search of another of its kind. I felt obsessive to have held onto these emotions towards a woman who did not know much about me, apart from my insecurities and subtle admiration for her.

The building with activities on each floor bustled with sounds that synced harmoniously. The energy was intensely packed, enough to lighten up the bright candle lit stairways on which people who had once been strangers interacted with each other. My mind paved the way as I wandered in between various conversations. Some stretched because they were leading nowhere but most stretched just so they could lead to a common place. Energy charged by our encounter ran through me, heating my body in the colder winds I walked against. The sweat from my face dripped, making these melting icicles the only souvenir left from the past shared moments.

Streetlights towered above creating two silhouettes around me, with a mute chaos playing in my head. Struck with an obsessive compulsion to replay what I should have said, I stalled, stuck like a deer in the headlights, looking at a dark image which was as familiar as a reflection in a mirror.

Cross-legged on a ledge, she balanced her left foot pivoting her swaying body. Her eyes gazed down to her laced up pencil thin fingers, making me envious of their placement. I have always been a firm believer that each path has a different story leading to a common goal and I didn't hesitate to wonder where I would have led myself if it weren't outside, standing opposite Rose. I had met her on 6 November, while the cool winds gifted by the sea in the Goan evening whispered for silence just so it could let me approach her peacefully.

Victoria Catherine Rose was 21 years old. She preferred calling herself just by her last name, which she had given herself as a teenager, disregarding her birth name which she never brought up. Her extravagant personality was in stark contrast to the simplicity in her looks untouched by makeup except for her kohl-lined green eyes. From the Hull, her northern English accent had hints of another one I couldn't figure out the origin of. But it was evident she had adjusted it to make herself easily understood the first time. We shared a common passion for travel. Having stayed in Goa for over five months, she knew the place better than I thought I did. Her travel plans were undefined because she wanted to make a living while living her life and India was her favourite destination. During our frequent encounters over the next few days she shared her life with me making me feel close to her from the very beginning. Her life became a familiar story and she told me about it. I reciprocated by teaching her about mine. Rose, or Victoria Rose as she liked to be called sometimes, had a lonely childhood with her grandparents. Her parents had had successful corporate jobs and were property dealers with homes all over the world. They received a lot of respect and wealth, enough to pamper Rose with a luxurious life. All this was ruined when her mother ran away from home with her share of the wealth and more. Greed made her ruin the rest of the family's lives through poor investments. Rose, didn't seem fazed by the struggle her life had been or the challenges it took to grow up after losing her old life before being given the opportunity to make another one. For a person who was deprived of love, she handed it out like free samples; I wanted to be a regular customer. She never mentioned her family again after introducing them to me. When I inquired why she wanted to reject her middle name; she said it had been her mother's Christian name—a constant reminder of the dark past that was the bridge between her middle and last names. She wanted no associations or reminders of a mother who had never seen her when she was a child. I was bewildered by her personality that took over my previously emotionless body.

I became a regular student at her dance classes; there was no improvement in my dance but significant advances between us. Four times a week I visited her class for eight sessions until we were left in the room by ourselves. This was the first time we were in a space with no eyes on us apart from our own; our attraction had crossed multiple levels from all the time we had spent together. Our excuse of being two lonesome travellers brought us in closer emotional proximity of each other. In truth, we both knew this impromptu connection had taken over our minds. The moment I fell for her, a million voices warned me about my emotions; they crashed over me, refreshing as a waterfall. My senses were hijacked, while my brain fell into the same chemical soup creating feelings similar to what I feel when I travel.

Red with the heat and embarrassment at my inability to dance, we both packed our bags, getting ready to leave. 'Will you be giving private lessons or will there be no more classes?'

She replied with sarcasm coating her mocking, 'I'm not good enough to help you out.'

The floor seemed to shrink as we found ourselves standing with our toes touching. Each word we spoke shortened the distance while the silence in the room nudged us closer. Our necks moved in unison as the door behind us rattled open to let us know we were no longer alone. Less than a breath away, she leaned in from her side to instruct me, 'You should lean in a bit more as you move.' As the door shut, I heeded her instruction to give into a kiss more passionately; it could be called the first of many.

A perfect relationship doesn't exist. However, that was a myth when it came to us. We both balanced each other's strengths and weaknesses well enough to make it hard to distinguish between the two. Despite growing closer to each other, falling into this was like deliberately walking into quick sand; we were us but still remained two different individuals. Initially it was like sitting on a seesaw. It was scary at first but we began to trust each other realizing that the other wouldn't jump off. Continuously competing with each other like teenage lovers, trying to outdo our feelings with every action and word shared.

Rose moved into my one bedroom apartment in Mapusa with me. The greenery around resembled a nursery in which, at times, I felt like an intruder with my brick walls. We gave each other nicknames that constantly changed but mostly I loved calling her Rose. A name as sweet as nectar that rolled off my tongue with ease. We traded each other's time and embarked on this journey together as guides. We were both foodies. When we didn't spend our time lying in bed till our bodies were stiff with lethargy we were out eating and discovering new foods. Goan food was a mouth orgasm, served in dishes that were waiting to echo the delight of the receiver. The elaborate and age-old recipes were complemented by coconut garnish, deeming this state a foodie's delight.

On the days we pretended to be explorers, we set out shielding our faces with caps to walk through heritage sites. The Church of St Augustine was a common favourite; we pretended to be archaeologists around the colossal high towers. The amalgamation of Portuguese, Indian and Islamic style were a treat for my camera, as was Rose, who posed in unconventional ways, continuously strengthening this dual admiration between us. On sunny days, we walked along the beach till the skies became orange while the swaying palms kept us cool in the warm weather of the day. We walked aimlessly but assuredly, knowing there would be a shack waiting to welcome us with drinks to refresh us and a meal to rejuvenate us.

Our time together felt like years of getting to know each other. We weren't even slightly daunted by the speed our emotions rushed at when they lingered on thoughts of the other. We were two friends when we spoke and one body when we didn't. Constantly learning newer passions the other had, covering the city like its fresh air, we ticked more items off our bucket list than we originally planned. Lily covered lakes watched us on our morning walks while we walked past bathing water buffaloes. Every local smiled with glee, making the start of every day fresher than the morning dew. The ambience hinted at a mini Porto and we both felt like teleporters stuck between two serene destinations.

Time began to tick by quicker than before. We had been together for over five months and soon what we had felt like it was as normal as breathing. Rose continued teaching Salsa while I sat at cafes writing when I wasn't clicking pictures. I was immersed in three of my most favourite passions. My book in progress was dedicated to her and the talent she brought out of me. We both knew that time was a constraint but our professional goals matched hand in hand with our relationship. We both wanted to be with each other, in Goa, the birthplace of our relationship; we chose to reside here.

There were several man-made wonders on our to do lists. Rose and I had places we crosschecked, an agenda we planned to finish. Soon there was no timeline to cover this because neither of us saw any end to this unexpected beginning. Nature was like a woman with no makeup, beautiful before and after, and that's what we wanted to admire.

It was February and the weather was perfect. In the clear sky the sun looked bigger than before. I had booked a day trip for the two of us to Panjim Jetty, where we'd spend her birthday in North Goa. Rose knew me well enough to have anticipated my thoughts and she pretended to be oblivious when I surprised her with breakfast and the news before we headed off a couple of hours after the sun had risen.

A cruise boat filled with tourists took us to the Monkey Islands over the clear cold Arabian Sea. I took pictures and stored them as memories, as well. I admired the beauty which I often collected on postcards. Soon all I could see was Rose. Her innocent smile while she enjoyed the smallest things in life. Her excited expressions as she watched the dolphins dance as they impressed her. She was the only magnificence that could compete with the scenery for my attention and soon the rest was meaningless.

We snorkelled, exploring the underwater life which was serene and had been well-preserved, much like the island we were on. Wet and cold, we walked over the beach, discovering the untouched trees, soaking up the sun. The salty wind blew while we walked slower every time our conversation led us to learn more about each other. Our feet were covered with white foam, wetting our sand-crusted bare feet that walked on in a disciplined manner. Soon our steps were in sync with our bodies and minds. The flowers around us appeared like they had been painted on a clean canvas. Its petals perfectly shaped contradicted that such perfection cannot be mirrored even by the finest artists. The sun rays blanketed us in warmth. The blue of the water was a perfect reflection of the sky. Like a perfect mirror image, enough to deceive an onlooker into believing there were waves creating ripples in the sky, it was impossible to tell when the blue skies ended and the sea took over. The night approached as these gentle waves attempted to outdo each other, one after the other. Each wave streamed over the other while we enjoyed our meal. As the night grew darker, the swirling sea seemed to become eager to spy on our rendezvous, getting closer to the shack where we were enjoying a barbeque. The package had immense value for money and was inclusive of all the treats, the highlight being Rose's company. We made plans for the future, disregarding any fears that they would not be fulfilled. We felt invincible together. I joked with a strong undercurrent of truth that we get married outside her favourite place in Goa, the Basilica of Bom Jesus. Outside the church filled with precious stones, the prominent design of a throwback to the Roman Catholic world was as attractive to her eyes as she was to mine. We discussed travelling to Mauritius and visiting the Giant Lily Botanical Garden and staying at the Ile Aux Cerfs Island. Her spontaneous attitude caused her to book it on her phone within minutes. I learnt how to use my MakeMyTrip points to book us a hotel to stay in. To her I was a 21-year-old in the pre-internet age for being oblivious about the convenient travelling application's features. She didn't know that it was the very same website that I had used to book my ticket which had led me to her.

We devoured our meal and were handed fortune cookies to end our dinner though we weren't eating Chinese food. Rose loved fortune cookies. She devoured them more for the unconventional taste and crunchy texture than the printed words. I opened the fortune cookie in front of her to read, 'Choose carefully what you hold onto, our hands might be big but our grip only tightens for a little.' I read the wise words to my unimpressed girlfriend, clutching her arm to put theory into practice.

'I'm big, not little,' her childish protest made her stand tall over me, making the point that she was a few more inches taller than me.

'You're tall, not big,' my set response fell on deaf ears as she snuck a piece of my vanilla flavoured cookie.

Rose's excitement had reached its peak over dinner. We had planned our first holiday despite living every day like it was one. The high waves showered us with sprinkles of the cold sea. Rose slept on a row of chairs like the others who had used up their energy at the island. Ever since we had been together, I didn't miss being alone and having time to myself. Our relationship was perfect for us, as we built steps together, climbing towards each goal. There were no awkward silences when she was around and this extraordinary feat reaffirmed that being together was perfect. I sat leaning against the wet life jackets looking into the darkness with nothing in sight. Couples wrapped their arms around each other, appreciating the time they spent together, while I couldn't be more thankful for those that Rose and I had spent.

'You seem to love that camera,' a pompous voice reached me louder than the crashing waves against our boat. A middle-aged woman dressed in formals, looking out of place on a cruise, stood up, inspecting me through her spectacled eyes. I smiled grasping my prized possession while its straps pressed against the back of my neck like a heavy garland.

'If you really love photography, what do you think about making money doing it?' she asked me in a matter-of-fact tone with a hint of an English accent looking at the cruise boat filled with tired tourists. I didn't answer quickly enough as she impatiently continued the one-sided conversation. 'Here's a card. We work in Bali. If you want to consider making money from your passion, call the number.'

The white card with a black design resembled a camera lens. 'How many more people have you fooled with this?' confused by the vagueness of this encounter, I read the bold name on the card; *Genesis Photography*.

'You might be the first,' she tittered and walked off into the dimly lit room filled with chairs, leaving me to ponder at the strange meeting.

Rose was the supportive backbone she had always been. We were committed to each other and she supported my thoughts that wavered between taking this job opportunity or staying in Goa and searching for another. I called the number on the sharp-edged card. A woman answered, sounding like an answering machine initially: 'Genesis Photography, how may I help you?'

'This is Arjun Talwar, I met with...' I realized I didn't even know the name of the woman who had handed this opportunity to me. Thoughts persuading me to disconnect the call arose due to the absurdity of this situation.

They were interrupted by the toneless voice. 'Yes, your name was mentioned. We were told you'll be coming in by the end of this month.' With the phone to my ear, I could hear the words that dictated a drastic change in my life. The deadline to my date of departure had been decided by a woman who I knew nothing about and it felt like she controlled the stability of my future with Rose.

Rose and I had to cancel our Mauritius trip but neither of us was upset. We were certain that going to Bali was a stepping stone to our relationship. I always knew I'd come back to her. I smiled at the irony of moving away from someone I loved.

I arrived on the scenic island of Bali with the confidence and the assurance that this distance will make our lives better in the future. I began to think like a new man, one with self-belief that Rose had induced. She helped me create my own path, with herself as my permanent destination.

I was usually a calm traveller but with a blink of an eye I

found myself prepared to live around two thousand kilometres away from Rose with no place to stay. Luckily her expertise and knowledge helped her use the points I had accumulated with my MakeMyTrip account to find a reasonably priced hotel in the surfing nirvana of Kuta to stay at temporarily. The Indian Ocean hugged the outline of Bali like a blue ribbon and I began my full-time job at *Genesis Photography* as a calendar photographer. After a week of work, I met with the woman who had gifted me with this opportunity to pursue my passion. She had returned from Goa and I envied her for that. For a woman who was supposed to be in her late forties, her face was as smooth as the white sands of Bali. She referred to herself as Ms C and never elaborated further. There was mysteriousness about her stern face and she spoke only when needed. There were rumours that she was an industrialist, a real estate tycoon and the owner of Genesis Photography, but she never took into account or disregarded the loud gossip she inspired. Despite the curiousness that surrounded her, she began to open up with me. There was generosity in her silent ways. She offered me a stay in her villa's guesthouse in Kuta. It overlooked the transparent, turquoise blue waters as it rested on a formation of large rocks. Time moved inversely than it did when Rose was around and I ticked each date off, moving ahead towards a life we had imagined in our heads.

I was kept busy being made to travel around the beautiful spots in Indonesia. My job entailed spending time travelling and taking pictures that I couldn't wait to share with Rose. All the time we spent apart was excruciating but Rose made me start looking at the future. I started to plan ahead and looked forward to a life we had worked for separately just so we could live it together. We both sat in different countries, by the beach, watching our favourite TV shows on the same day, just to shorten the distance between us. We sat watching the moon shine on either side of the world; the distance between our bodies was a lot but not enough to impact us when we spoke to each other.

I was taken to several destinations around the exciting island. From the Ubud Monkey Forest to the local shopping that reminded me of Goa, the beaches were my favourite place to shoot and spend time alone. On days I missed Rose more than I could bear, I covered miles without realizing it. I knew she was, too, but I didn't want to fluster her just like she never flustered me. Being close to the water and the wet sand was the closest I could get to her, while being so far away. I'd walk along the shore watching water caress the beach like a mother caressing her newborn. Seagulls glided in the air, guided by the gentle ocean breeze. Seaweed and plants rooted firmly were washed, looking greener each time, like Rose's rainforest green eyes that glimmered more than the sun-kissed sea. My back was warm from the sun rays that beamed straight at me, while my feet stayed cool from the showers of the resting waters that slowed down at my feet. I looked as far as I could till I had to create what I couldn't see, getting lost in these short moments where there were no people, no chaos and no technology, just nature and its closest friend, enemy and child.

From being a heavy and selfish sleeper, taking up the whole bed, I had learnt how to make enough space for her, on the outer side of the bed because the inside made her feel 'trapped' as she justified herself. The nights I surprised myself by sleeping, I lay on my side resting against the wall, while my unconscious body adjusted in the hope that Rose might join in. I wrestled against the nights, trying to find comfort in the dark until the light burned my eyes. Despite heavy work days, my brain worked faster, concocting scenarios to fulfill in the future. It seemed sleep had divorced itself from me. My body lay comfortable in thoughts until the yellow street lights were replaced by the natural, white light. Surrounded by a pile of pillows, my breathing pattern did not vary because she wasn't shuffling near me to cause these patterns. While I lay, a lingering haze of sleep in the back of my mind, I would create images out of each shadow that went past the wall outside my window.

My work made me familiar with my surroundings; the familiar smell of the beach making me feel nostalgic. I worked long hours, spending twenty-four hours at a time with Ms C who monitored my work like a hard taskmaster. She appreciated my photography; I knew that because she told me that as frequently as my camera shutters closed to capture a moment. Soon, it became evident she wanted much more than my work. I spent hours in her villa's studio, constantly aware of her staring at me while she sat on her expensive chairs, blatant about her actions. We didn't speak much. She commanded me and like her subordinate I followed, ignoring the unnecessary stroke on my shoulder each time she leant down a few feet away from my face to whisper. She loved the moments I captured through my lens, disregarding the ones I shared from when I was back in Goa. I sensed jealousy prick her like a thorn each time I brought Rose up.

She introduced me to the several clubs in Bali. From night clubs like Vi Ai Pi to brunches at Nikki Beach. Her hospitality turned from generosity to a selfishness and desire. I didn't reciprocate. She would wrap herself around me every time we went out. I didn't want to lead her on. I lived my life before being led on by false assumptions about the future; it wasn't a pain that any medicine could cure. With each passing day, I started to learn more about her. She reigned over everyone like a queen. She was the prima donna of Bali. She had it all and everybody was in debt to her. Like a bank, she controlled the lives of all those who invested their time in her life. I soon became a bait she was reeling under and I continued to tug hard to let go. I was hooked and soon all the help she lent me became a debt, my time as the collateral.

Ms C began to share more about herself with me, as though I was her personal diary. She spoke of her desire to travel the world because she found beauty in the idea of escape. She loved Asia but it was already hers, she claimed stamping her authority over it. She asked me to visit Turkey with her and only after several repeated requests did I realize her forceful offer was not a joke.

It had been six months since I had come to Bali. Rose and I were not avid users of social media messaging but we compromised, adopting instant messaging. After constant persuasion, I submitted my papers to finally go back to India. Rose gave me a homecoming gift by emailing our previously cancelled tickets from MakeMyTrip. It had a one word subject: Uncancel. With no incurred cost, we retrieved our tickets and eleven months into my gap year, my life began to make up for all the disappointments that had tried knocking me down.

'I think I've landed in a postcard!' A good morning message from Rose, injected me with ecstasy. After constant convincing and being skeptical about visiting Bali, Rose was here. I was leaving my job at *Genesis*.

I reached before time with the aim of leaving earlier to

take her around the Bali I knew she'd love. I couldn't wait to guide her at the beaches where boats sailed in the distance on cold waters gracefully slicing through the waves. The water would glisten trying to match up to her face. I sat at my desk, doing my work, impatient to cover miles, losing track of our footprints till the moon started to shine brighter than the sun.

Ms C didn't come in for work. She was usually annoyingly early. The rest of our expansive studio was empty apart from myself and the wet, developing photographs. Her phone was unreachable and nobody answered the phone at her villa either. I heard a creaking sound as her secretary opened the door.

'Where is Ms C?' I asked sourly.

'She sold her share of the company; yesterday was her last day,' the words sounded like some foreign language, causing my confusion to lead to an evident irritation in my voice.

'Catherine's daughter has come to Bali. They're meeting for lunch today.' I felt lost like a child assigned algebra for the first time. Confused with the news that had been announced by her assitant.

'Catherine? Who? Who's her daughter?!' I cried out, clueless.

'She's gone to surprise her daughter, Victoria Catherine Genesis...' Her words caused me to have a piercing nightmarish realization. I fled out the door, to return to the villa. The door to my guesthouse accommodation was left with a note. 'Where the old meets the new, where the ancient meets the contemporary, where Asia meets Europe. The place I love is where you'll find yours.'

The letter sucked the air out of my lungs. Lifeless, limp and cold on understanding I had been the hook to reel Rose in. I was deprived of the basic necessity of love and now this greed had caused me to lose mine. The only information Rose had from me was my address to Catherine's villa. With no local number to call from, she only knew the address for the one person she ached to wipe out of her memory; her mother, Catherine Genesis. I was wide awake, experiencing my worst nightmare and there was no escape from it. Imprisoned with this truth, I felt weaker than ever and yet determined to fight for the cause that might already have been lost.

Catherine, was an obsessive woman who got everything she demanded. I was the one thirst she couldn't quench. Love has no boundaries; like a jungle it is beautiful yet scary to get lost into and I was stuck in the middle.

Rose had lived most of her life hiding her name and identity only to meet the reason for her hiding. Now lost in the land of the Ottoman Empire, I flew to Turkey; I was once again fulfilling one of Catherine's several demands.

Terrified, of the reality of this being a never-ending search seemed to sink in. The nights were long before she was gone and now the days will compete with them. I am frightened to narrate this truth. I persuade myself by lying to say it will all fall into place, for once. I knew from now on, my eyes will remain open like the entrance to a tunnel, with the hope that she would be standing on the other side, waiting.

I was lost in the openness of Istanbul. The vastness of this amalgamation of cultures was my map to search for Rose. In search of breadcrumbs to return to the past, I felt like I was lost in a blizzard not knowing which direction I should go in. It all appeared to be a blur. My moist eyes ached, seeing her face in every individual who looked like a crude outline with no other face but Rose's. I searched like a hopeless wanderer for months with not a glimmer of hope. I only had our memories to hang on to. The sound of howling winds symphonized with the voices within that echoed her silvery voice. As my mind pretended to identify her in every alternate passer-by, my heart would stop, frozen as the landscape. There were days I thought she didn't swirl in my brain like the blood in my veins only to realize that with each breath, her name was the oxygen to my body.

My entire life has been a losing game of hide and seek. I constantly lost out on everything that was dear to me. But like an addict, I returned to the itch that tears me from within. Everything I loved left as though adhering to a fixed schedule. These chain of events have killed my capacity to think logically. Lost in the cocktail of endorphins which ended in sorrow, my past wounds seem fresh with the sting of hopelessness of a never-ending search. I search away from the beaches constantly reminding myself of our morning walks, during which I had admired her as she had admired the scenery. My feet glued to the ground, prevent me from losing track. My mind is filled with insane laughter knowing it's too late. We had to part ways even though we wanted to be together. The irony of our actions, which would lead to our ultimate goal of being together, blinded me into believing this distance was the ideal way to move ahead. Now I am here in the bustling streets of Turkey's capital admiring its beauty. Hundreds of people walk hand in hand, taking pictures of the Blue Mosque and famous cats that dot the city where east and west meet. I seek solace and oblivion from the times that pierce me each time I ponder over moments that passed quicker than a blink of the eye.

I travelled the world. I saw places; I used to touch the globe, just to pretend I was there. The easy access and affordability led me to meet new people. But all I wanted was the old. Life stops for nobody, we all have to race ahead. The average time a man can sprint a hundred metres is fourteen seconds and those who can go faster, get to walk at the end. But we end up crawling, begging for death. Some beg for it to come and some don't.

We all leave souvenirs with whoever we meet, in the form of memories. She had left me with a shop full of them; with each blink of an eye, I saw a new one. Just as they begin to repeat themselves, it starts to sink in that she isn't here and the only new memories I will have are these that I will have to recreate. Today, I sit alone and soak in the beauty my eyes were used to being presented with every morning. Today I sit alone, accepting the truth with each tear.

I scroll through each message of ours. I go through past Facebook messages from the very start before we had accumulated four thousand three hundred and forty two honest conversations. Sharing videos that reminded us of each other. I started from the very first message I had sent her. Her voice clearer than mine; I hope it remains that way. I relive each of these read messages like watching a film. I keep sending messages with the hope that soon they will be read. Reading the progress we made. From the first time she surprised me by making me perform a dance that I thought I couldn't, to helping me achieve more than I would sign myself up for.

We meet people in our life so that they can lead us to other places and people. Rose was the destination I wanted to reach. She defined beauty. I loved touching her skin, feeling her pulse, stroking her wavy hair, just to keep reminding myself I wasn't dreaming. Her charisma fuelled me to succeed beyond measure. Her aura hypnotized me into believing I was better than I really am. She made me more confident about myself, a canon shooting me into the right direction. Life is as unpredictable as the weather and today I wish I had heeded that fortune cookie and grabbed onto what had meant the most. Our minds had fit better than puzzle pieces from the same box. Connected, we spoke without speaking and laughed without thinking. She was in every blink of my eye. If only I had known my fate would not change I would have warned her from before. All I have left is a picture in my wallet and an album of collages in my head.

#Unexpected Turn

Sanil Sachar's journey from being a young student-cum-footballer to an author of two books at 23 years of age had started rather unexpectedly. Miles away from his family and friends, studying and playing football in the north of England, Sanil started writing during breaks in his football matches. The pen got mightier and the author in him got hungrier. The result was *Summer Promises & Other Poems*, his first book published by Rupa Publications in 2013.

When he finished writing his second book, an idea he had for long started taking shape. He wanted to do something that presented young writers with an opportunity to publish their work. He shared his idea with Rupa Publications and they co-created the contest 'An Unexpected Turn'. Powered by *Hindustan Times*, India's leading English national daily, the contest encouraged writers to submit their short stories on a microsite as well as on social media with only one condition: the story needed to have a twist. The contest reached a staggering eight million people online and received an overwhelming response.

Sanil along with senior editors from the *Hindustan Times* assessed the entries and were pleasantly surprised by the energy and expression of the young aspiring authors. After endless discussions and debates 'The Other Man' by Jaiveer Singh Hundal emerged as the their top pick.

The Other Man

*T*here were two kinds of people in Martyr Town: the diseases and the diseased. This city was in desperate need of a cure. A cure that was located at the corner of 'nowhere' and 'definitely not there'.

The streets of the southern quarter were old, made of bricks as though awaiting a horse-drawn carriage that was not likely to come again. Ancient structures lined these avenues, crumbling and decaying, forgotten in their ruin. The streetlights flickered, tired, waiting to pass into the shadows, much as everything around them had already done.

There were places where people stood beside one another as equals. Not here. Here they formed a line. The putrid stench of autocracy lingered in the air. The rich were rich and the poor were hungry. After all, hunger begets sin and sin is business. Gangs and cartels could be found on every street in the southern quarter. Their wares were expensive.

For those who lived southeast of the city centre, debt was currency. When a city did not progress, it stagnated. A gentle push in the wrong direction had sent half the city back into the dark ages. A simmering had ensued, a few sparks were re-ignited in trying to reclaim what was left of the ruin, but the blanket of ash had swept those few under, leaving behind the city's cold, dark corpse.

It was here, in this part of the city that the best stories were told. Alias Alamos didn't believe all that was said in stories, but he did think that they had basis in some modicum of fact. If you looked close enough, you could part the legs of a story and uncover the truth hidden inside.

He had been born and brought up near the factories in South Station. His father had been as poor as poor could be, his mother had been as absent as absent could be. She would sit on the couch every day, the radio on, listening to whatever it was she listened to with a needle sticking out of her arm. On especially lean days, when she wasn't numbed by the constant need for self-medication, his mother would appear, briefly, to caress his hair and kiss his cheek and tell him what a beautiful boy he was. That would last until the other woman possessed her. Withdrawal, that woman was called. Withdrawal took over when the sun went down, when she bit and scratched and screamed and pleaded until her needs were fulfilled. Only when that was done would she go to sleep in front of the radio, and his mother would go with her.

His father had been a small-time peddler of drugs. He had started out as a promising prospect for the ZiZi family, but that had all gone to hell when he got caught sampling his own wares. From then on, he did odd jobs. These were hard to come by, because the ZiZi family had burnt away half his face with hydrochloric acid. They'd poured it over his skull and held him as he screamed. His wife was the only one who could stand to be around him after that. Her constant sedation probably helped her to stomach his appearance. Alias wondered if his father had deliberately promoted her use of drugs to keep her from leaving him.

Finally, his mother had died in her sleep; his father on the front porch. The old man had been standing there, waiting for a drop off when he'd been shot between his eyes. Knowing Martyr Town, the bullet was probably still embedded in the door, right where his head had been.

The town almost always had storm clouds hanging over it. It rained more often than not, and the forest on the eastern border had grown wild as a result. 'The Grey Garden,' it was called. Because of the mist that hung over it. People swore that there were animals beyond the ordinary in the old woods. A load of tosh in Alias's opinion. Those who saw anything out of the ordinary rarely lived to tell tales about it after all.

11.30 p.m.

Alias limped down a shadowy avenue, his face bloody and his right arm dislocated from its socket. He couldn't help but wonder what it would have been like if he had gotten out sooner. Fear, he believed, had driven him in and it had been fear that had allowed him to fight his way out. Yet one final act of self-defiance had to be committed before he could be truly free.

With his weaker left arm, he whipped out his six-shooter and aimed it around the corner as he entered the alley. The gesture turned out to be a hollow one; there was nothing but a cat purring in the shadows. As he made his way down the alley, he reflected upon the night that had passed.

6.30 p.m.

He was being framed, he knew. The traffic was sparse, so he barrelled down the streets.

They'd found his fingerprints at the crime scene, but he hadn't killed his wife. The others didn't believe him. Why would they? He was an ageing detective at the end of his rope, dangling by the final bristles of a life that had cost him more than it had given. Unfortunately, his fingerprints hadn't been the only bit of evidence. His boots had been found at her apartment as well, covered in her blood.

He fumbled in his jacket pocket, one hand still on the wheel. Fishing out a small bottle full of his migraine medication, he popped a couple of pills and swallowed them with spit. He would not be getting much sleep tonight and the pills would have to do to keep his throbbing head in check.

In his arrogance, the killer had left a clue at the crime scene. It was more of a taunt really, something the killer knew only Alias would find odd: an old ticket to the Vicar's fair, that took place at the southern-most tip of the city. What rattled Alias was the date on the ticket: 15 July 1993. The fair itself had been abandoned almost ten years ago, when the authorities decided that it wasn't safe. The rides were getting old and accidents were becoming increasingly common.

Whoever had left it had been very thorough. Not only were they framing Alias, but they had also done enough research into his past to know what would make him tick.

Alias was a bundle of indignation and fear when he reached home. He had barely gotten to the door when his sight began to blur. He reached out to the railing to stop his fall, but his arms began trembling from the strain and he fell to his knees, darkness overcoming him.

He regained consciousness when the first few drops of rain hit his face. The sky had turned grey, as though to match Alias's mood. He shook his head, clearing it of the wailing that had washed over him. He always heard that horrible shrieking when he blacked out. Then the darkness would roll over him and he'd collapse. When he got it checked, the doctors had found nothing wrong with him. They'd prescribed medication for a number of maladies, but nothing could seem to get rid of it. The darkness always found him.

He got off the wet concrete and staggered indoors. The blackouts were proving to be a hinderance. They had grown in frequency over the last couple of weeks and today of all days, he couldn't afford to be weak. He grabbed a bag from under his bed and proceeded to the basement. There, he walked over to one of the loose floorboards in the corner and pulled it up. Below was a metal box. He carefully removed it. He retrieved a gun from within and checked it for bullets before putting it in his bag. He also stashed away a smaller box of extra bullets.

He was putting the metal box back into its hiding place when his phone buzzed. It was his partner, the rookie cop who had recently been transferred from somewhere upstate. The naive boy was the only one who believed Alias hadn't killed his wife. The others...they would arrest him the moment they laid their hands on him. There was no place for a bitter old cop in the new guard. The veterans were getting flushed out to make way for younger, fitter cops.

Alias let the call go to voice mail. He'd check it in the car on the drive to the Vicar's Fair. Today would be the day. Today was July the 15th.

He got into his car just when the rain began to fall in earnest. Alias carefully drove out of the garage; the rear wiper wasn't working and rain-swept glass was a treacherous ally at best. The fair ticket seemed hot in his right pocket. The years had made it frail, and the thing was almost torn in half where a lazy clerk at the ticket booth had probably clipped it by mistake.

He drove down the expressway wondering what would be waiting for him at the fair, whether he'd survive it. A part of him hoped that he wouldn't. He didn't have an awful lot to live for. The road was slick with water and his car skid just a little as he drove over a bump at full throttle.

The fair was situated on a large, circular expanse of land surrounded on all sides by high cliffs. The only way in or out was through a narrow tunnel which burrowed through the base of one cliff. The tunnel had a two way road, but it was still barely large enough for two cars to pass each other. The lights had stopped working due to the lack of maintenance and graffiti adorned most of its dark stretch.

Alias emerged into what had once been a parking lot. There didn't seem to be anyone else here. The ticket was still in his pocket, and he held onto it, checking to ensure that he had come to the right place. His head began to feel heavy again and he cursed himself for being so weak.

And then he saw it.

He could feel the rumbling of Alias's car through his bones, such was his anticipation. The tunnel they had driven through had been dark and dank, the breath of abandonment wafting over his neck as he passed. He hid his car in the parking lot, stashing it behind a pile of rubble and making sure it was out of sight. Alias was weak, he could sense that. This would be easier than he'd anticipated. Who wouldn't believe that a depressed detective, who was being investigated for the murder of his own wife, would come to the most secluded spot in the city now? This was the site of Alias's daughter's death, which had happened all those years ago. He remembered it as if it were just yesterday, the crumpled little body of the girl at Alias's feat. They had both been at the fair that day. Alias did not know it, but their little feud had gone back years, decades. It would all end today.

He pulled out his revolver and approached the gates of the fair.

Alias, his own weapon at the ready, was walking through the breezy, rain soaked fair, his jacket was soaked through and a light shiver running down his spine. The weakness had not left him yet. Alias cursed and walked on, his gun held out in front of him. He'd spied the other car in the far corner of the parking lot and had in turn hidden his own car in an attempt to maintain the element of surprise. As he approached the ferris-wheel, a large lump formed in his throat. A little to his right, there was a slight rise in the ground level—a small hump of sorts. It had been at that very spot that his life had turned upside down. For a moment, he couldn't feel his fingers, as the grief overwhelmed him with the force of a bomb. He gasped for breath, his whole world spinning as night turned to day and the small hump took on the broken form of his daughter, lying spreadeagled in a pool of blood, wearing the summery yellow frock with the pink bow that she had loved so much.

Grief is a powerful ally to those inflicting it. The stricken are often paralysed and thus made easier and so much more fun to dismantle. Alias had shown not a modicum of emotion since the death of his daughter, a tragedy that had resulted in his marriage falling apart. Now he was a sobbing mess, weeping for a past he could not change. Pathetic.

The gun was cold in his hand. It would be almost too easy to end Alias at that moment; but suddenly, there was the sound of footsteps approaching.

Alias heard them too, along with the click of the safety being turned off a gun. He silently moved for cover, positioning himself behind a wooden structure that might have been an outhouse once upon a time. The footsteps came closer and Alias moved slowly along the length of the low wooden wall to the other side, trying to get a look at whoever it was. The man he assumed to be the perpetrator of the hellish crime was, from what he could see, wearing a black hooded jacket that fell to his knees. His gun was held out before him; he was inching to the other end of the wooden wall, the end where

Alias had first hidden. It was going to be a close call, but Alias would have to move away the moment the other man crossed the wooden wall, or he'd be found out.

Holding his breath, Alias waited for the man and then, silent as a ghost, he pivoted around the wall to the other side. He was about to slouch into another shadow when the man came back around the wall. He'd been toying with Alias. He now had his gun raised, which to Alias was a declaration of his intent. Without delay, Alias whipped out his revolver and shot at the figure, but the man moved out of the way. However, he grunted, leading Alias to believe that his bullet had at the very least grazed him. Firing another couple of rounds to keep the other man at bay, Alias raced back towards the parking lot. His head was still aching and if he blacked out now, he'd be at the mercy of a mad man.

He grounded his teeth in frustration. Who was the other man and why was he interfering? He knew Alias well, and it wasn't hard to imagine that he had more than a few enemies. He raced through the rainy fair ground, intent on getting to his target if it was the last thing he did. One way or the other, this would end tonight.

Alias hopped into his car and drove through the parking lot and down the tunnel, his head now heavier than ever. He could hear a car behind him. The other man was following him in the same car that had been parked in the corner.

Alias was in trouble, big trouble, but no one would get in the way of his plans. He would be the one to take care of Alias, no matter how many complications he'd have to get rid of along the way.

The road was slippery and his car was skidding at every turn, and the only consolation he could draw from this was that his pursuer would be inconvenienced in a similar fashion. Relief lasted only for a moment, before his eyes shut and the darkness swallowed him again.

His car hit the curb and the front left wheel struck a fire hydrant. The car flipped over and landed upside down, Alias still inside.

Alias crawled out of the wreckage. He couldn't feel his right arm and something was dripping over his eyes and into his mouth. Blood. The onlookers were shocked as he got up and half-ran, half-limped down the shadowy avenue towards an alley.

The man chasing him stopped half a block away and got out of his car. He walked in the shadows to avoid attracting any unwanted attention to the gash on his right arm. He walked towards the wreckage but by the time he got there, a huge crowd had gathered. Alias was crawling out of the wreckage, looking rather worse for ware. A glance in his direction, however, was enough motivation for the injured man to move faster. By the time the man chasing Alias could push through the crowd, Alias had disappeared.

11.30 p.m.

Alias limped down a shadowy avenue, his face bloody and his right arm dislocated from its socket. He couldn't help but wonder what it would have been like if he had gotten out sooner. Fear, he believed, had driven him in and it had been fear that had allowed him to fight his way out. Yet one final act of self-defiance had to be committed before he could be truly free.

With his weaker left arm, he whipped out his six-shooter and aimed it around the corner as he entered the alley. The gesture turned out to be a hollow one; there was nothing but a cat purring in the shadows.

He climbed the steps to his house, leaning heavily on the railing with his left arm.

It was all he could do not to pass out on the steps, completely exposed. He limped through the doorway. Locking the door behind him, he fell with a thud against it, the gun in his hand. He cursed himself silently; the box with the extra bullets was in the upturned car. He had three bullets in his gun, and now he'd have to make them count. Two psychopaths, three bullets. Not the best odds, but not impossible ones either.

Alias thought he was alone in the house, that the wooden door protected him from all the bad people outside. He was a fool. Leaning against the door, the weak, pathetic remnants of the man who had been such a promising detective enraged him even more than it had ever done before. It would be over soon though, and there would be no more anger.

Alias caught his breath and struggled to his feet. The blood was beginning to impair his vision. He'd have to take care of it before it became another impediment.

Splashing water on his face, he managed to remove most of the blood and reveal the true extent of the damage. There was a deep gash on his forehead. He reached into the cabinet behind the mirror for a bandage and wrapped it tightly around his head. It was difficult to do this with just one functional arm. He then reached into the pocket of his jacket for the bottle of pills, but it wasn't there. It must have fallen out during the accident.

He cursed again, just as he heard a loud crash from the living room. His front door had been broken down. He sank on his knees at the side of the open bathroom door and waited. He heard footsteps walking along the corridor and took a deep breath. Without another thought, he pulled back the hammer of his gun and dove into the corridor, squeezing the trigger as he did so. His bullet found its mark, right in the forehead of the other man.

Alias slowly got to his feet. Finally, he would see the face of the bastard who had ruined his life. The man had fallen face first to the floor, and the hood was still up. Alias approached slowly and yanked it back. He gasped. It was his partner. The fool had been following him and now he'd have another murder to his name. He walked back to the bathroom to redo his unraveling bandage. The little fool had gotten himself killed out of curiosity, he told himself. Alias felt guilt, but no regret. His life had been at risk and he'd taken a call.

Alias had taken care of the pesky kid and now it was his turn to die. The man smiled as he stepped over the body and made his way to the bathroom. It was time to end this acquaintance.

Alias spat into the sink and opened the cabinet to take out another bandage. His gun was in his left hand. He shut the cabinet to look at himself in the mirror again. That was when he saw him.

The man in the mirror had a gun pointed at his head. Alias took a deep breath and looked him dead in the eyes. What scared him more than the man with the gun was the little girl by his side. She wasn't a day older than ten, wearing a summery yellow dress with a pink bow in the front. He looked back up at the man and finally understood. He had found the strength to do what he had craved to do for years. He smiled and nodded. The man holding the little girl's hand put the gun into his own mouth and pulled the trigger.

Alias blinked once and fell back, unseeing, unknowing.

Alias had accepted what had to be done, and after all those years of hatred, he finally felt some amount of respect for the other man. They had started this journey as one and now, they had found their way back to one another.

What a journey it had been.